# Flying High

# Flying High

ANNIE DALTON

An imprint of HarperCollins*Publishers*

To Sally Beets, and to
Gemma and Madeline of
Westborough Community School,
all undercover angels

First published in Great Britain by Collins in 2001

Collins is an imprint of HarperCollins*Publishers* Ltd,
77–85 Fulham Palace Road, Hammersmith,
London, W6 8JB

1 3 5 7 9 10 8 6 4 2

The HarperCollins website address is:
www.**fire**and**water**.com

Text copyright © Annie Dalton 2001

The author asserts the moral right to be
identified as the author of this work.

ISBN 0 00 675486 4

Printed and bound in Great Britain by
Omnia Books Limited, Glasgow

# Chapter One

Last week I went back to Earth to visit my family.

OK, so it was just a dream, but it was totally true to life.

It was Christmas and my little sister was helping Mum to decorate the tree. I was amazed how much Jade had grown. She's getting to be a proper daddy long legs like me, I thought.

Apart from my sister's gangly legs, everything was exactly the way I remembered; the tomato-coloured throw on the sofa, the daft DJ rabbiting away on the radio, spicy chicken smells floating from the kitchen. Even the Christmas decorations were the same, right down to the painted wooden angel with glittery wings.

Perhaps Jade read my thoughts, because she took the little angel out of the box and suddenly she went all tearful. "Melanie's an angel now, isn't she, Mum?" she sniffled.

They glanced towards a framed photograph on top of the TV. It was one I'd never seen till now, which isn't that surprising. Des, my step-dad, took it on my thirteenth birthday, only hours before a speeding joyrider booted me out of the twenty-first century and into the next world.

Then I took another look at the photo and came out in major goosebumps. It was that look in my eyes. So dreamy and far away. Almost, well – wise. As if I *knew* what was going to happen. I felt a flicker of awe. Was it possible that as Des shouted, "Say Cheese!" and clicked the shutter, that I was actually secretly preparing to leave Earth?

Jade tugged anxiously at Mum. "My sister's an angel in Heaven, isn't she?"

Mum tried to smile. "Of course she is, pet."

My throat ached in sympathy. My mum thought she'd lost me for ever. She thought I'd vanished into a meaningless black hole called Death. I was suddenly desperate to tell her that dying wasn't like she thought. "Don't be sad," I whispered. "This might be hard to believe, but I really am an angel! I go to this special angel school and I've got angel ID. And I've made these brilliant friends..."

At least, that's what I tried to say. But the instant I heard my own voice – POP! My old home vanished like a soap bubble.

My ears filled with a vast mysterious throbbing, like a cosmic humming top. And all at once I was whooshing through space, past glittering stars and planets – and woke, gasping, in my room at the Angel Academy.

I felt genuinely shocked, like a castaway washed on to some far distant shore.

It's weird the things I miss, now that they've gone for ever. The way my little sister smells of warm wax crayons. The sound of Mum's voice. The taste of her cooking.

I sat up and took a few deep breaths. Heavenly air has this incredibly sweet, delicate scent. It reminds me ever so slightly of lilacs, but there's nothing on Earth quite like it. I was feeling better already.

Then I looked out of my window and saw the soaring skyscrapers of the Heavenly City, all sparkling and shimmering in the celestial light, and the last traces of homesickness melted away. I felt a blissful smile spread across my face. "*This* is your home now, Melanie," I whispered.

Yippee! It's the weekend, I remembered suddenly. No school for two days!

I wiggled my toes, admiring my glittery toenails. Lola had let me use some of her precious twenty-second century nail polish.

Omigosh, Lola!!

I hunted frantically for my clock. Yikes! I'd really overslept!

I grabbed the phone and tapped in Reuben's number. "Are you awake, Reubs?" I asked breathlessly.

I heard a familiar chuckle. "Pure angels don't need to sleep, remember? Unlike some people I could mention."

"Yeah, yeah, don't rub it in," I wailed. "Look, I'll have her down at the beach in two ticks, I swear."

"Wait!" Reuben sounded slightly panicky. "What's that thing I say to her again? Happy many returns? It sounds slightly bizarre."

Unlike me and Lola, our angel buddy has never lived on Earth, so concepts like birthdays leave him seriously confused.

But while we were chatting, I caught sight of my reflection in my crumpled PJs, and practically freaked! I was organising a top secret party and I wasn't even dressed yet! I totally did not have time to coach

Reuben in human birthday etiquette. "If it worries you, don't say it," I gabbled. "Just give her a flower or something. Later, OK?" And flinging down the phone, I sprinted for the bathroom.

Sorry, you're probably totally confused by this time. Isn't this girl Melanie like, dead? you're thinking. That means she's gone to live in Heaven, right? So how come she's still nattering about nail varnish and parties? Isn't that just a teeny bit, well, shallow? I know, I know! I've been at the Angel Academy for almost three terms now, and I still have NO idea why I was picked to be a trainee angel. It's not like I showed signs of unnatural saintliness in my former life. My teacher, Miss Rowntree, thought I was a total bimbo.

Of course, I prefer to think she was mistaken. I like to picture some celestial talent scout passing through my hell-hole comprehensive (bravely trying not to inhale the pong of school chips and cheesy gymshoes), when suddenly she sees me, Melanie Beeby. And it's like, "YESS! She's the one!!" Don't ask what I'm up to at this crucial moment. Probably in the back of the class, texting a mate, or in the girls' toilets, agonising over my latest pimple.

But whatever stupid thing I'm doing, this scout is totally not fooled. With her angelic super-sight, she zooms in on me in massive celestial close-up. Closer, closer, until BINGO! She sees clear through to the real, the essential, Melanie, with all her unusual and unused abilities. Qualities just like, *wasted* on someone like Miss Rowntree.

Ah well, I'll probably never know how it happened. The great thing is I LOVE my incredible new life. And like Lola says, who said angels can't have fun! (Lola is just her human name by the way. We only use our angel names for like, official purposes. Mine's Helix if you're interested.)

I met Lola Sanchez, otherwise known as Lollie, on my first day at the Academy and we clicked just like that. It was like we'd each found that special best friend we'd been missing, ever since the universe began, if that makes sense?

We even have almost identical taste in clothes. (Though being from the twenty-second century, Lola is that *tiny* bit more outrageous.) We're genuine soul-mates. Sometimes we actually read each other's minds.

Can you imagine what a nightmare it was, trying to keep my telepathic soul-mate's party under wraps!!

I'd been planning it for weeks. Reuben was in charge of the music. Thanks to me and Lola, he's shaping up to be a fantastic DJ, creating fabulous fusions of heavenly and terrestrial sounds, like you would *not* believe.

I'd managed to persuade Mo to do the catering. Mo runs Guru, one of our favourite after-school hang-outs. They do gorgeous party food there and I wanted to celebrate my soul-mate's birthday in style!

After the fastest shower in the entire history of showers, I threw on my bikini and matching sarong, fastened a gold chain around my midriff, tied a funky pirate bandana over my hair and beamed at myself in the mirror. I looked delicious, even if I did say so myself!

Grabbing my beach bag, I raced down the corridor to knock on Lola's door.

Lola opened it instantly, looking so hopeful that I felt like a real traitor. But I just said "Hi" and all the birthday sparkle went out of her eyes.

"Oh, hi," she said in a gloomy voice. "Did you want to borrow something?"

I *hate* keeping things from Lola. I sternly reminded myself that I only had to string my best mate along for a teensy bit longer, and gave her my brightest smile. "Sorry to bother you, babe, but I was hoping you'd help me out with this project?"

Lola looked more depressed than ever. "Oh, right."

"I won't blame you if you say no," I wittered. "It's going to be really boring. Mr Allbright wants me to do this stupid survey for Science."

She shrugged. "It's not like I've got anything better to do."

"You're a star! Erm, maybe you should change into some beach clothes first," I suggested cunningly.

Lola frowned. "What kind of survey is this?"

"Oh, who knows!" I babbled. "Mr Allbright said I had to find a rock pool. I'm meant to observe the microscopic lifeforms and take notes."

I was on safe ground here. Mr Allbright is always saying stuff like that.

"Oh, all right." Lola vanished and came back wearing a bikini top, hipster shorts and a stylish cowboy hat. She struck a cover-girl pose. "Will the teeny-tiny lifeforms approve, do you think?" she said in a bored voice.

"They'll go green with envy," I said truthfully.

But underneath I was panicking. We were running *really* late.

By the time we reached the sea shore, Reuben was slumped on the jetty, twiddling his tiny dreads. He sprang to his feet. "Finally!"

"What are you doing here, Sweetpea?" Lola demanded.

"Me?" he said innocently. "Oh, I came to help Mel."

As a pure angel, Reuben is physically incapable of

telling lies. But he's getting quite good at kind of *editing* the truth.

He jumped down into a little glass boat which was tugging gently at its moorings. "Are you girls coming or what?"

Lola looked puzzled. "You never said anything about boats, Boo!"

"Oh, duh!" I put an imaginary pistol to my head and did my best airhead giggle. "Yeah, Mr Allbright said I had to check out this special rock pool which you can only get to by boat." I secretly crossed my fingers, adding brightly, "Don't come if you don't want to, Lollie."

"Oh, for Heaven's sake," she sighed. "Let's all go and observe the thrilling rock-pool creatures."

Phew! Phase One of Operation Lollie was successfully completed. But I didn't know how much longer we'd be able to keep this up...

## CHAPTER TWO

Reuben is a real water baby, always messing about with boats and surfer gear. So he did all the technical steering stuff, which left us free to do the film-star bit, trailing our hands in the spray and admiring the tiny fish darting in and out of the coral.

But I couldn't exactly enjoy myself, could I? Not with Lola being in such a huff. Several times I came close to cracking, but that would have ruined my big surprise.

Ever since I arrived at the Academy, Lola had been going on about this totally luminous beauty spot and how she couldn't wait to see it for herself. But as we sailed closer to the shore, I started to lose my nerve. When you get down to it, it's just sand and water, I thought. Can sand and water really be that special?

Actually, yes.

As we dragged the boat up out of the water, Lola suddenly went silent.

Lacy little waves lapped at the edges of sand so pure and glittery white that it looked as if the beach was strewn with powdered diamonds. Palm trees waved lazy green fronds in the sweet-scented breeze. Tiny parakeets zoomed to and fro, shrieking to each other as if they owned the place, which I suppose they kind of did. There was no doubt about it, Treasure Beach was the tropical paradise of your wildest dreams.

Lola gazed around her with a dazed expression. "This is Treasure Beach, isn't it?" she said at last.

I tried to sound offhand. "I've no idea. It's just where Mr Allbright said to go."

Her brow crinkled. "But why? There aren't any rock pools!"

"You noticed that too!" I said at once. "Darn! Mr Allbright must have meant us to check out the other side of the island!"

I saw Lola's expression change. "Does anybody live here?" She was staring at the sand.

Reuben and I shook our heads energetically. "Uh-uh."

"So how come there are all these footprints?"

I did a double take. "You're right! How weird!"

Lola started moving stealthily towards the trees, concentrating so hard on her big mystery, she totally didn't see what was right in front of her.

"Any minute now," Reuben whispered.

We heard Lola gasp. And when I saw what Mo had done, I gasped too, even though the whole thing was originally my idea!

In an airy shelter, thatched with palm leaves, was a little desert island café. Everything was beautiful: the snowy tablecloths, the exquisite place settings decorated with tropical blossoms. And overhead, in the shadowy branches, I caught the faintest glimmer of fairy lights.

"Ohh," I breathed. "This is just so sublime!"

I mentally fast-forwarded to the end of the party, with everyone dancing in a twinkly fairy-light haze. If only Orlando could be here, I thought wistfully. Then it really would be perfect.

But I didn't have time to feel sorry for myself, because just then all our mates jumped out of the shadows yelling, "Surprise, surprise!" They unrolled a massive banner with, "HAPPY BIRTHDAY LOLLIE!" in rainbow-coloured lettering, and people started throwing glittery confetti.

"I don't believe it!" Lola shrieked. "You monsters!"

I heard a chink of ice and there was Mo, his bald head gleaming, wearing a dazzling white apron over Bermuda shorts. He was holding a tray of drinks. He handed one to Lola and she went into fits of giggles.

Mo's special birthday cocktails were WAY over the top! Shocking pink fruit juice, crammed with fruit and flowers and topped with a cheesy paper parasol.

"Happy birthday, Ms Sanchez," he said calmly, and began unpacking goodies from a huge cool box.

Reuben had obviously taken my advice literally, because he totally skipped Lola's birthday greeting. Instead he seized a huge pink blossom from one of Mo's place settings and stuck it in her cowboy hat. "Have a lovely time!" he said shyly.

He ran off to do something to the sound system and Lola's favourite song came floating through the air.

I suddenly heard myself say, "He's looking so much better, isn't he?"

"Yeah! If it wasn't for the scar, you'd never know."

Not too long ago, Reuben came with us on his first ever trouble-shooting mission to Earth. Unfortunately he ran into an old enemy of mine, who gave him a really savage beating. Luckily we found our angel buddy in the nick of time, and the Sanctuary staff did a great job of patching him up.

"I still can't believe Brice used to be an angel." I had to close my eyes. Just saying his name made me feel as if I was dropping dizzily through space. "I mean, how does a total sleazeball like that make it into the Angel Academy? It doesn't make sense."

"I keep telling you, Brice left the Academy *aeons* before our time. Just forget about him because you're never going to have to see him again."

I shuddered. "He acts like we've got this bizarre cosmic connection."

"In his dreams! Just remember, you got the better of him, not the other way round." Lola pulled a face. "Anyway, what kind of angel are you, girl! Plotting parties behind my back! And why didn't you invite that beautiful boy Orlando?" she added, giggling.

I sighed. "He's gone missing again. No-one seems to know where he is. Anyway, I'm completely over him."

"Yeah, right!"

"I mean it this time." I took Lola's drink and handed her a carefully gift-wrapped box. "Happy birthday, babe!"

Her face lit up. "Boo, you shouldn't have!" (I have no idea why Lola calls me Boo. She invents mad nicknames for everyone.)

But before she could even tear off the paper, there was an outbreak of earsplitting bird calls. All the local parakeets left the trees in a huge screeching flock.

Everyone looked blank, then our mates started groping in bags and pockets. One by one we found our pagers and switched them off.

"Hey, Dino!" Reuben called. "Take over the decks, will ya?"

Lola handed her parcel to Mo. "Mind keeping this till I get back?"

"No problem. Perhaps you'd like to grab a snack?" Mo's eyes twinkled. "Who knows when you kids will eat again!"

We hastily helped ourselves to various goodies.

"Ever consider a change of profession, girlfriend?" I teased.

Lola took a last slurp of her cocktail. "No way!" she protested. "Enjoy my party, you guys!" she yelled to her remaining guests, and we raced down to the shore.

Minutes later, a flotilla of glass boats went skimming back across the water. That's how it is in the angel business. When you get the call, you drop what you're doing and just take off. No-one minds, in fact it's just the opposite. You know that someone somewhere needs you and let me tell you, that is an incredibly cool feeling!

# CHAPTER THREE

When I first arrived at the Academy, I just could not understand why Lola was so desperate to get into the history club. I mean, who in her right mind would *choose* to memorise diagrams of the medieval strip field system?

But studying history at the Angel Academy is totally not like that.

Still not convinced? OK, then check this. At *my* school, we get to travel in time!

I know, I know, I couldn't believe it at first either. But now I'm completely into it. Last term, Lola, Reuben and I actually signed up to do history as our special subject, which got us on to the Agency's books. I am now totally convinced that being a time-travelling trouble shooter is what I was created for!

That's the thing I love about this school. On Earth they make you wait until you're grown up before you can do anything interesting. But here, you constantly get dropped in the deep end, which is scary but also incredibly exhilarating!

So even though we'd had to bale out of our own party, I was wildly happy. And I could tell the other trainees felt an identical mix of nerves, excitement and jittery pride. From the shore, the sight must be totally magic, I thought.

The Agency had called us and we had answered and now we were leaping from wave to wave like dolphins, in our tiny glass boats filled with light...

"Wonder what this is all about," said Lola, bringing me out of my dream.

"Must be serious for them to page us on our day off," said Reuben.

Simultaneously Lola and I looked down and wailed, "Omigosh!"

Neither of us had thought to bring a change of clothes!

"Great," I groaned, "I've got to go time-travelling in a silk sarong and sparkly flip-flops!"

"Oh, and hipster shorts and cowboy hats are so much more suitable," quipped my soul-mate.

Reuben gave us a pitying look. He wore his usual tragic tie-dyed top and cut-offs. Style is yet another Earth concept which baffles our angel buddy. But like Lola says, "Sweetpea is so chilled on the inside, he can totally get away with it!"

We'd barely set foot on dry land when a sleek limo purred over the sand towards us. We jumped in breathlessly. The driver executed a stylish U-turn and went bombing back downtown to the Agency.

When I first got here, that word really used to bother me, making me think of poker-faced men in suits, masterminding huge cosmic conspiracies. It's true some agents are a teensy bit poker-faced. And they do wear gorgeous suits! They also move in deeply mysterious ways. But hey, they're angels. What do you expect?

Officially we're known as "celestial agents" these days. But most people still affectionately refer to the Agency building as Angel HQ. It's the tallest skyscraper I have ever seen incidentally. And every few seconds you see brilliant bursts of light overhead as agents zoom back and forth.

I slid out of the limo, and snatched a moment to admire the Agency tower. It's made of some special celestial-type glass which constantly changes colour.

Two more limos drew up, letting out a stream of angel trainees. They hurried in through the revolving doors, waved their IDs at the day staff and sprinted for the lifts. Reuben spotted our friend, Amber, on the other side of the doors, and instantly went in to join her. I could see her hopping on the spot, desperately trying to put on her trainers. Like everyone else, she'd sensibly changed her outfit on the way over.

"I can't go in like this!" I moaned to Lola. "I look like a refugee from a cheesy package tour!"

She looked shocked. "Melanie, we're off to save planet Earth. Who cares what we wear?"

My jaw dropped. "You really think it's *that* huge?"

She laughed. "No, you dope, I was kidding! It's probably yet another boring drill to keep us lazy trainees on our toes."

I tried to decide if this would be deeply disappointing or a major relief. Before I could make up my mind, Lola disappeared through the Agency doors, cowboy hat, hipster shorts and all. This didn't leave me much choice. Adjusting my slipping sarong, I sashayed into the cathedral-sized foyer, flashed my ID, and followed my mates into an unusually crowded lift.

"Anyone know what's up?" I asked, as we went humming up to the top of the building.

Amber was carefully braiding her hair into a perfect fish-tail plait. That girl is *so* organised it's not true. "I heard they'd got a problem in ancient Egypt," she said through a mouthful of grips.

"Egypt? No way!" scoffed a boy from our history class. "First World War, someone told me."

The lift doors slid open and we hurried down gleaming corridors to the hall I remembered from our Dark Study training. Michael was there already, conferring with someone on an invisible ear-piece. As well as being our headmaster, Michael is a major big cheese at the Agency. He's so gentle and approachable, it's really easy to forget he's an archangel. Then he fixes you with those terrifying archangel eyes, and it's like he sees right into your soul.

He stepped up to the mike and we all fell silent.

"Sorry for calling on you at such short notice," he said. "As you know, the primary function of the Academy is to train the celestial agents of the future. Normally we only send trainees into the field for educational purposes. But in times of extreme cosmic necessity, we have to call on trainees to provide support for an existing task force."

Woo! I thought. Maybe they need us to save the planet after all!

"A unique situation is unfolding in thirteenth-century France," Michael went on.

Lola waggled her eyebrows at me. Trainees know that "unique" is well-known Agency-speak for "dangerous".

"Normally, when we identify a trouble spot, we send in divine personnel to liaise with local angels. On this occasion, we sent in a small team of highly experienced senior trainees. I'm sorry to say, we underestimated the scale of the problem."

Michael paused, scanning the rows of silent trainees. "Our young workers are in danger of being completely overwhelmed by local conditions and urgently need back-up. Unfortunately, all our trained operatives are tied up elsewhere, which is why I called you here today."

A ripple of excitement went around the hall.

"You'll be leaving shortly. The maintenance crew is just running last-minute checks on the time portals." Michael paused. "It's only fair to warn you that this crisis could go on for days. I know some of you have exams."

The seniors gave theatrical groans.

He smiled. "We'll try not to disrupt your studies too much, but until this situation is resolved, you'll just have to catch up on your school work between shifts. Is that clear?"

Everyone nodded eagerly.

"Of course, this is an excellent opportunity for those of you who haven't previously visited Earth, to experience the, erm, realities of earthly existence," Michael added mischievously.

All the regulars exchanged world-weary grins. Our headmaster was teasing us about the down-side of time-travel, which is basically mud and poo!

Like everyone else, I complain madly about time field trips, but apart from the icky smells, I secretly adore them and I learn *heaps* more than I ever learned from history books. OK, it's not all corsets and castles, not to mention I invariably ruin my best trainers. Plus when we get back, Mr Allbright makes us write a humungous report! But boy, do we write fabulous essays!

"Anyone here know anything about the Children's Crusade?" Michael asked in a casual voice.

Now try not to die of shock, but it just so happens that I knew heaps about this bizarre historical episode. We'd just finished studying it with Mr Allbright. But naturally I had no intention of saying so. I have a complete phobia about speaking in public. Anyway, at my old school, only sad try-hards like Venetia Rossetti spoke up in class. But Michael just gave me one of his humorous all-seeing looks, and said, "Melanie, perhaps you'd like to fill us in?"

I stood up gulping with nerves. Everyone stared at me expectantly.

"Erm," I said. "Well, it all started with this shepherd boy. Oh, did I mention he was French?" I quavered. "I didn't? Well he was, he was French. And he had a vision. At least, that was his story!" I added darkly. Everyone laughed. Hey, this isn't so bad, I thought.

I ploughed on bravely. "News of this vision, or whatever, spread like wildfire, and suddenly thousands of other kids were leaving their families, their ploughs, their herds of goats and whatever, to follow Stephen."

I noticed a new trainee studying her nails and deliberately pitched my voice a little louder.

"Maybe that doesn't sound like a big deal," I said. "But what you have to realise is that in those days, kids had absolutely no freedom. Even rich kids were like their parents' *chattels*, their property in other words. As for peasant kids, they were put to work practically as soon as they could toddle. So they never had one spare moment to stop and think like, 'is this all there is?' OK, so Stephen's project was completely insane, but the fact that the kids got as far as they did makes it an incredible achievement."

"What was this project exactly?" someone asked.

"They planned to march all the way to Jerusalem where a big holy war was going on."

All the pure angels looked amazed. "A holy war?" said one. "Are you kidding?"

I sighed. I hated to admit that humans were still murdering each other in my own time, on the grounds of religion. So I just said, "No, I'm not kidding. These holy wars were known as the Crusades. Now, like you guys, Stephen thought all this killing was wrong. He believed a kids' crusade could win their enemies over with love, a really radical idea back then. Unfortunately," I told my audience dramatically, "the whole thing went totally pear-shaped."

"Thank you, Melanie," said Michael in a firm voice. "That was most informative."

Ow, I thought. I was just getting into it!

He launched into the usual pep talk. We were not to attempt to be heroes. We were members of a team, links in a divine chain, blah blah blah.

Then we all had to zoom off to Departures, where we collected our Agency insignia. They're like little platinum tags you wear round your neck, to show you're on official business. Tags also help us stay in touch with the Agency, via the Link (that's sort of like the angel internet).

To my relief, I managed to squeeze into the same portal as Reuben and Lola. I always get massive butterflies before take-off. My worst moment is when that glass door slides shut. Like, EEK! The point of no return!

Then I heard Reuben humming our private theme song. "You're not alone," it goes. "You're not alone…" And I instantly felt myself relax. I was going time-travelling with my best mates. What could be better?

"Can you believe we're going to medieval France!" Lola burbled.

"I can't believe we're going to France full stop," I said truthfully.

She looked shocked. "You've never been to France? But it's so close to England."

"I know, but Mum never had any money, did she?"

At that moment our portal lit up like a royal firework display and we were blasted into history.

Time-travel, Agency style, is incredibly smooth and speedy. Just a few minutes after take-off, or several centuries earlier, depending on which time system you're using, I stepped out on to my favourite planet.

We were in a river valley somewhere in the south of France, totally surrounded by rolling hills, making me feel as if I was at the bottom of a massive misty blue bowl.

To judge from the position of the sun, it was somewhere around midday. The heat was phenomenal and the air was filled with the busy ticking and scraping sounds of zillions of little insects.

It probably sounds really sad, but I was totally over-excited at being in a foreign country! And even though this was Earth, not Heaven, the air smelled fabulous. I think the heat was bringing out the scent of all the wild lavender and rosemary growing everywhere.

Lola frowned. "Have you seen that river? It's way too low."

"Looks like a major drought," Amber agreed. "See all the cracks in the dirt?"

I'm a city girl myself, so I don't pretend to know about stuff like dirt or average rainfalls or whatever. But I did notice that the valley had a bleached, stone-washed look, as if all its bones were getting a bit too near the surface.

I'd gradually become aware of faint surges of noise drifting down the hillside. Soon, I was able to make out individual sounds. The dumty-dumty rhythm of drums, the toot of flutes and wave upon wave of sweet young voices singing some medieval hymn.

I felt a shiver of excitement go down my spine. My mates and I exchanged awed glances.

*They're coming*! I thought excitedly.

Tiny figures appeared over the rise – first a trickle, then a stream and finally a flood of marching children.

We stood totally stunned as the child crusaders straggled over the hill and down into the valley. Tattered blue and gold banners fluttered over their heads, their bright colours wavering in the intense heat.

"Omigosh," Lola breathed. "I had no idea there were so many."

Some of them were just little tots and had to be carried by the older ones. None of them appeared to own a pair of shoes. Their feet were in a terrible state. Yet they limped along, singing with heart-rending beauty.

The first kids into the valley instantly spotted the glint of water. Everyone broke ranks and went rushing down to the river to drink, bathe their feet, or simply cool off.

I found the scene really disturbing, to be honest. It reminded me too much of refugee camps I'd seen on the news in my own times. Michael's right, I thought. This situation is way out of control.

Reuben nudged me. "Uh-oh! Lollie's run into some local personnel."

I saw Lola chatting away with an Earth angel in medieval dress.

Eek, I thought. Don't think wimples will make a comeback!

I think the Earth angel was equally startled by Lola's outfit, because I heard Lola say, "*Oh pardon, madame!*" And she started explaining how we'd had to leave Heaven in a hurry.

This is *so* cool, I thought. They were speaking in medieval French, yet I understood every word! It's one of the perks of being an angel, and it still gives me a major buzz. If Miss Rowntree could only see me now, I grinned to myself.

Then my heart almost stopped beating.

A dreamy-eyed boy was making his way towards us through the crowd. His T-shirt and jeans were so faded by the sun that I could only just make out the familiar angel logo. It had been too long since he'd had a haircut and he looked completely shattered. But I'd have recognised him anywhere.

It was Orlando.

# CHAPTER FOUR

Now I'm not, repeat *not*, one of those tragic girls who go yearning after boys who don't even know they exist. But you can't tell a heart what to feel, and my heart was secretly hoping for a teeny tiny sign that Orlando was pleased to see me.

But he didn't even smile. "What happened to you, Mel?" he demanded rudely. "Get lost on your way to the beach?"

"Erm, actually we're your back-up," I mumbled. "The Agency paged us in the middle of Lollie's birthday party."

I was genuinely shocked. It is SO not like Orlando to make hurtful personal remarks. He is usually on this totally higher plane.

Did I mention that Orlando actually looks like an angel? Well he does; a soulful dark-eyed angel in an Italian painting. Officially he's still at school. But he's such a genius that the Agency is constantly sending him off on major missions. Unfortunately I only tend to run into him when I'm flouting a major cosmic rule or generally acting like a ditz.

I think Orlando guessed he'd upset me because his expression changed. "Sorry if I overreacted," he said awkwardly. "It's great to see you guys, honestly. It's just that we're a bit overstretched as you can see."

"Tell us what you want us to do," said Lola.

I don't think I've ever seen Orlando look so depressed. "It's a nightmare," he sighed. "Stephen's totally convinced these kids they're going to witness a miracle. When they reach Marseilles, the sea will part and they'll walk across dry land all the way to Jerusalem."

"It isn't going to happen, is it?" Reuben said softly.

"No. And I'm not sure how they'll handle the disappointment. So I'd appreciate it if you guys could keep your eyes and ears open. That way we can nip any trouble in the bud. Apart from that, just do what you can for them. The little ones especially."

We set to work. The children were in such bad shape that they soaked up healing angelic vibes like blotting paper. The pure angels, in particular, couldn't get their heads round what they were seeing. "Why would a little kid put himself through so much suffering?" one said in horror.

"Most of them probably didn't get much TLC at home, remember?" I pointed out.

Reuben whistled through his teeth. "I don't believe it. They're on the move again."

All around the valley, exhausted children were gathering up their pitiful possessions, getting ready to go back on the road. It seemed like we'd given them just enough strength to press on to Marseilles. Of course, without food and rest, the effects of their angelic energy transfusion would soon wear off. But even if the kids had understood this, I don't think they'd have cared.

Reaching Jerusalem, that's all they cared about.

We marched on through the simmering heat. An old man came out of a tumble-down hovel to watch. He shielded his eyes as the never-ending procession tramped past. The sight seemed to upset him. "Go home and help your fathers," he called.

"We have but one Father," a girl replied through parched lips. "And he is in Heaven."

I tried to imagine my mates on Earth getting all steamed up over some weird holy crusade. Queuing for tickets for a pop concert maybe, or even doing some hilarious fund-raising stunt. But these kids were putting themselves through hell for an *idea*. Some of them were literally dying on their feet. Forget going to Jerusalem. They'd be lucky to make it to the docks. And it really upset me.

"Give me five minutes alone with this Stephen," I muttered. "I'd give him a vision he wouldn't forget in a hurry."

Orlando gave a tired laugh. "Be my guest!" He pointed back up the track. A covered cart was rattling in our direction, stirring up swirling clouds of dust. The cart was painted in the same vivid blue and gold as the banners and hung with fluttering blue and gold pennants.

Three kids shared the driver's seat, taking it in turns to sip from a leather flask. A posse of teenagers on horseback rode alongside. They had the wary expressions of professional bodyguards.

From the way the other kids cheered and tossed their dusty caps in the air, it was obvious this mysterious Stephen was the medieval equivalent of some big rock star.

Suddenly someone yelled, "Tomorrow in Jerusalem!"

The cry was taken up in a great roar. "Tomorrow in Jerusalem! Tomorrow in Jerusalem!" Once it had started, the cry went on and on, wave upon wave of sound crashing on my ears.

"Tomorrow in the cemetery, more like," said Lola grimly.

I puffed out my cheeks. I'd only been here a few hours but it felt like a lifetime. Poor Orlando had been coping with it for weeks. There and then I made a secret vow to do everything I could to help him. I'll be totally professional, I thought. Then Orlando would see me in a completely different light.

We were getting closer to the port. The air had acquired a fishy smell, along with the familiar olden-times pong of sewage and rotting garbage. Except for an occasional horse-drawn cart rumbling along on clunky wooden wheels, there wasn't much traffic. It was too hot for sensible folk to be out. But the children went marching on.

We had left the countryside behind by this time, and the dirt track had turned into narrow cobbled streets. Medieval tenements loomed up on either side of us, like gloomy great canyons, blocking out the sunlight. A sleepy murmuring came from behind closed shutters. It seemed like the locals were waking from their afternoon siesta. But as they heard the kids approaching, doors and shutters flew open.

Everyone wanted to see this extraordinary procession.

Orlando caught us up. "This is where things could get ugly." I could hear his tired voice going up the line, keeping the overworked trainees on their toes.

It was obvious he was expecting major trouble. But the people were really sweet, clapping and calling out encouragingly, as if the kids were athletes at the end of a marathon.

A girl leaned out of an upstairs window and started throwing flowers. The idea quickly caught on and suddenly rose and jasmine petals were raining down. The children marched on through falling blossoms, their eyes feverish with excitement.

The cart with its outriders had moved to the front by this time, the bright flags and the sound of drums and flutes all adding to the party atmosphere. Some kids actually found the energy to turn cartwheels and somersaults. The childish singing echoed eerily around the walls of the medieval tenements. The whole thing was dreamlike and deeply disturbing. Then I realised why.

"Omigosh, this is like that story!" I whispered to my mates. "The Pied Piper or whatever."

Reuben didn't know the fairytale, and by the time I'd reached the part where the spellbound children followed the mysterious piper into the countryside, never to be seen again, the cobblestones ran out. And there in front of us was the hot dazzling blue of the Mediterranean.

Ships, like elaborately carved wooden castles, rode at anchor, their sails tightly furled. Sailors climbed up the rigging as nimbly as if they were just going upstairs. Others were unloading sacks and barrels, or ferrying small rowboats back and forth across the harbour.

Marseilles is only just across the water from Morocco, and the dockside smells of rope and tar were deliciously mingled with exotic spices and the scent of foreign perfumes.

I had no *idea* the Middle Ages was so multicultural! The whole world was there: black, white and golden-skinned seamen, all cheerfully fraternising with local tarts and gangsters, not to mention Arabs and Africans in dazzling ethnic clothes.

This is *so* cool, I thought. Just in time I remembered I was supposed to be on duty. Stop being a time tourist, Melanie, I scolded myself. You're supposed to be looking out for trouble.

I didn't have far to look.

A boy emerged from inside the cart, shielding his eyes from the glare. He was dressed in what was once a white tunic, with an extra bit of grubby white drapery trailing over his shoulder. His wispy gold hair badly needed a wash.

Now personally, I would never recommend the guru look, unless you've got a brilliant suntan. And after months of travelling through sweltering heat, in a cart with no springs, this boy was the colour of sweaty cheese.

But style wasn't nearly such a biggie then, and the instant he appeared, I heard excited whispering, like wind blowing through grass. "It's him, it's Stephen!"

Adults had joined the crowd by this time: sailors, fishwives, priests and local tradespeople, all dying to see this famous youth for themselves.

Stephen made his way to the front of the crowd, where his minders had improvised a stage from a plank and a couple of barrels.

He sprang lightly on to the platform, and gazed peacefully down at the crowd with eyes that were just that little bit too blue. Later Lola said it was almost like his eyes had literally been dazzled by his glimpse of Heaven. Like he saw how the world *could* be, not how it actually was.

He started to speak and everyone hushed at once. Speeches all sound the same really, don't they, but I think the gist of it was that the medieval adults had screwed up big time and now it was up to the kids to put it right.

Then he stopped talking and it went electrifyingly quiet. Stephen gazed dreamily down at the crowd with those disturbing Heaven-dazzled eyes and thousands of awed sweaty faces gazed back. Well, it's not every day you see a kid with his own hotline to Heaven, right?

Suddenly Stephen swung to face the ocean, whirling his arms like wings, yelling, "LET THE WATERS PART!" And at that moment, with his gold hair and drapery, he did look alarmingly holy.

"He believes it, doesn't he?" I whispered to Orlando.

"That's what's so scary," he whispered back.

The crowd held its breath, waiting for their miracle.

And absolutely nothing happened.

No thunderclap, no bolt of lightning, no waves scrolling back like curtains. Nothing.

First his followers just seemed bewildered, but as the moments ticked past, they looked totally panic-stricken. Several started weeping and tearing at their clothes. Some even fainted. I saw Stephen's minders muttering to each other, probably feeling like dopes for believing him in the first place.

Poor Stephen just looked as if he wanted to crawl away and die.

Two richly-dressed merchants were watching all these goings-on with close interest. One had a thick shock of silvery hair and a smile which never quite reached his eyes. He slung a fatherly arm around Stephen's shoulders.

"Don't lose heart, boy," he told him encouragingly. "My name is Gervase de Winter, and if you are willing, my friend and I may be able to help you. Miracles come in many shapes and disguises."

The men explained that they owned several ships. By a strange coincidence, two were sailing to Jerusalem in just three days' time.

When Stephen finally grasped that they were offering to take them to the Holy Land for free, I truly thought he was going to burst into tears.

I wanted to be pleased for him, but I couldn't help feeling suspicious. The merchants didn't strike me as the holy type somehow. I mean, what was in it for them?

In all the confusion I'd lost sight of Reuben. Suddenly he came flying out of the crowd looking terrible. He spotted Lola and they had an agitated conversation, then next minute Reuben went flying off again.

I ran over to Lola. "What's up?"

"Mel, Reuben heard those guys talking. Those ships aren't going to Jerusalem. They're planning to sell the kids as slaves."

"No way!" I gasped. "Someone's got to tell Orlando!"

"Reuben's gone to tell him now."

And then, as if there wasn't enough going on, a cosmic fire alarm went off in my head. I'm sorry, it's the only way I can describe it. Angels constantly pick up vibes which humans don't even register. But I'd never experienced this particular horrible silent jangling before.

I saw Lola clutch at her ears, almost losing her balance.

"What's going on?" I hissed.

She shuddered. "It has to be the PODS. A juicy slavery scam would be just up their street."

The official Agency term for the Powers of Darkness is the Opposition. My mates and I call them the PODS, private shorthand for the gruesome beings who constantly try to sabotage our work on Earth. Unlike angels, PODS have no actual shape of their own, which unfortunately means they can disguise themselves as pretty much anything or anyone they fancy.

Luckily a routine scan revealed absolutely no evil cosmic personnel in the vicinity. Then I clocked some children standing slightly apart from the crowd.

"Lollie, bet you anything it's those kids!" I hissed.

We moved in for a closer look and the jangles immediately doubled in intensity.

"Well, that's weird!" I said. "I mean, they're not PODS, so they've got to be for real, right?"

Lola frowned. "I'm not sure. Don't they look just a teensy bit too clean to you?"

She was right. They looked more like child actors in a movie set in the thirteenth century. Nice shiny hair. No sores, fleas, or pockmarks. Costumes miraculously free from grease and grime.

But it was the humans themselves who really baffled me. They had a quality I've only seen in angel kids. Nothing to do with being good or saintly, but a kind of lovely inner glow.

The kids *definitely* weren't behaving like angels, however.

"If we don't get a question about this in the exam, I want a full refund, de Winters," one boy complained.

"Yeah, Dominic," his mate chipped in. "I can't be doing with this religious garbage. To think I paid money for this."

From the way everyone was glaring at him, I decided that Dominic must be the intelligent-looking kid in the stylish medieval cap.

"Come on, you guys!" he said despairingly. "I'm giving you a unique experience. Real live history is happening right in front of your eyes. So stop moaning and give it a chance!"

Lola and I exchanged puzzled glances. What was going on?

"Admit it, Dom," said one of the girls. "Stephen's a total nut."

Dominic sighed. "Agreed. But give him some credit. Before Stephen came along, these kids were like dumb animals, blindly following orders, half asleep. But Stephen woke them up. He made them see things could change for the better." There was real excitement in Dom's voice.

"Oh, who cares," another boy whinged. "This place stinks."

A girl with freckles turned on him. "Of course it stinks, you bozo. History's supposed to stink. Anyway, that Roman arena stank to high heaven and I didn't hear anyone complain."

"Yeah, but the gladiators were lush!" one of the girls giggled.

I'm only giving you the gist of what they said. They were talking really rapidly in a weird slang which is quite tricky to translate.

"Come on, Dom," said his freckled sidekick in disgust. "Take these losers back to school."

Dom fumbled inside his jerkin, fishing out

something that looked like a miniature mobile phone and hit several tiny keypads.

The air started to flicker. Scribbles of colour appeared, weirdly superimposed over thirteenth-century Marseilles; colours so wild and futuristic, I couldn't even tell you their names.

At that moment Reuben came to find us. His eyes grew huge with awe. "Is this actually happening?"

"You tell us!" I squeaked.

The scribbles formed into ropes of light, all twirling at different speeds. As they twirled they emitted confused crackles and bleeps, like someone tuning an old-fashioned radio.

Dom watched tensely, as the ropes twirled faster and faster. He seemed to be counting under his breath. "NOW!" he yelled suddenly.

And as if they were playing some bizarre skipping game, the children dived through the ropes – and vanished!

# Chapter Five

I finally found Orlando in the middle of some big meeting with the local angels. I have to say, he didn't seem too thrilled to see us.

"This had better be important, Melanie."

"Oh, it is! We've come to report a major time anomaly!" I burbled.

I felt quite proud of myself. Mr Allbright had explained all about anomalies last term. But of course brain-box Orlando had to go one better.

"What kind?" he said at once.

I sighed with irritation. "Duh! Some kids who totally shouldn't be in this century, that's what kind. Like, they belong to another time?"

"They were from the future, definitely," said Lola.

"I'd say some time around the twenty-third century."

Orlando shook his head, "You're mistaken. The Agency put a ban on human time-travel until at least the twenty-fifth century."

"So?" I said. "Someone's obviously broken the ban."

"You did say to tell you if we saw something unusual," Reuben pointed out.

"Unusual!" I snorted. "That's the understatement of the year!"

Orlando darted a nervous glance at the Earth angels, who weren't looking too impressed at having their meeting interrupted by three over-excited trainees in beach wear. "What exactly do you think you saw?" he asked in a low voice.

I was practically jumping up and down. "We don't just *think* we saw something, OK? We registered a major cosmic disturbance, which we traced to a bunch of time-travelling kids in medieval outfits."

"Suspiciously pristine outfits," Lola chipped in.

"Way too pristine," I agreed. "One boy activated some kind of device and he and his mates jumped through some kind of worm hole or something and vanished."

Orlando looked desperately stressed out. "Look, I can't deal with this right now. As you can see, I've kind of got my hands full as it is."

Don't think I wasn't sorry for him, but we'd stumbled across something potentially huge and I knew it. "So, you're going to just like, pretend it never happened, is that it?" I demanded.

Orlando shut his eyes and took several deep breaths, while I tried really hard not to admire his incredibly lovely eyelids. And when he opened them again it was like our conversation had never taken place.

He called cheerfully to a passing Earth angel: "Lucius, meet Melanie and Lola! Think you can put them to work?"

If Lucius thought our clothes were weird, he had the good manners to keep it to himself. "But of course," he smiled. "It will be my *plaisir*."

Orlando shifted swiftly into trouble-shooting mode. "The slavers won't dare to kidnap these kids in public," he explained. "And the ships don't sail for another three days. If we all pull our weight, there's a chance some of the kids will change their minds about going to Jerusalem."

"Will you please follow me," Lucius asked politely.

I flashed him my most professional smile. "Sure!"

But inside I was seething. Why, oh why, wouldn't Orlando take me seriously? I've made a few mistakes in my angel career, I admit. That time I materialised to a human without permission, for example. Oh, and I once sort of *whacked* an Elizabethan human, accidentally activating his hidden angel powers. OK, so it was William Shakespeare, but it all worked out brilliantly in the end. Yet Orlando insisted on treating me like this major fluff-wit.

But in the angel business, as you know, your private life totally has to take a back seat. Actually it was quite a relief to throw myself into work. As well as the actual kids, we targeted local adults. Like Lucius said, some of them must know the slavers' true intentions. And a cosmic nudge from a celestial agent just might inspire them to tell the kids what was really going on. We even zapped the evil merchants themselves. Well, it was worth a try!

In the end, Lola and I got so blissed-out on cosmic energy, I think we could have happily gone on all night. Lucius had to tell us our shift was over.

"I don't know 'ow we would have manage wizout you," he said.

"He's *so* charming," Lola whispered.

Unlike some, I thought bitterly.

Orlando came to see us all off. "Thanks, guys! I'll see you tomorrow, yeah?"

I gave him the briefest possible nod. But he turned to talk to his colleagues, never even noticing he'd been blanked.

We blasted back to Heaven in a blaze of white light.

"I want to sleep for a week," I moaned. "Plus I want you to swear you'll never let me go on a field trip in flip-flops again."

Lola looked dazed. "Uh? Oh, sure."

"Are you OK?" I asked her.

She gave me a faraway smile. "Just trying to remember something."

Minutes later we were handing in our angel tags. We dragged ourselves through the Arrivals bay and out into the street, where a fleet of Agency limos waited in the heavenly twilight.

All the way back to school, I was longing to fall into bed. Yet after a long hot shower, my tiredness magically disappeared.

I looked at my nice clean PJs on my pillow and I thought, "Nah!"

And I went into a mad whirl of activity. I threw on jeans and a cropped T-shirt, splashed on my favourite fragrance (it's called Attitude, and comes in the cutest bottle) and grabbed my new beaded clutch bag.

I was just on my way to find Lola when she appeared in my doorway, wearing an almost identical outfit.

"The Babylon, right?" she grinned.

 52

We slapped palms. "The Babylon!"

And giggling like idiots, we rushed downstairs and out of school.

These days, when we need to unwind, we head straight for the Ambrosia district and dance ourselves silly at the Babylon Café. It only opened a few weeks ago, and already it's the coolest club in town.

We'd just checked in our jackets when Reuben turned up.

"I don't suppose you're up to dancing," he teased Lola. "Now you're such an old lady!"

"Hey, buddy, I can dance you off your feet any time!" And Lola dragged him on to the dance floor.

I hadn't seen Reuben dance since his run-in with Brice, the cosmic outlaw. It was great to see him behaving like his old mad party-animal self.

After several dances, we went outside to cool off. The gardens at the Babylon are unbelievably lovely, designed so that they literally seem to float in mid-air.

We found a private little arbour, all overgrown with passion flowers, and sat sipping ice-cold fruit punch, gazing up at the glittering fields of stars overhead. For some reason I started thinking about Stephen. What was it Dominic had said? *Before Stephen came along these kids were like dumb animals, blindly following orders, half asleep...*

Suddenly Lola blew out her breath with relief. "Oh, finally!! I've been going nuts trying to think where I'd seen them!"

I shook my head. "I've no idea what you're on about, babe."

"Duh," she said. "Those weird FX. What did you think I meant?"

I gawped at her. "You've seen them before! Do you know where?"

"Sure, babe! On the news."

I couldn't believe my ears. "You mean in your time?"

"Six months before I got shot," said Lola calmly. "My grandmother was just about to dish up her famous *fajitas*. My brothers were fighting over the TV remote as usual. My grandmother said to cut it out. She wanted to watch a current affairs programme. She switched channels and there was Bernard de Winter talking about how time-travel was finally—"

"De Winter?" I interrupted. "That is *so* bizarre. I never even heard that name before today and now it's cropping up all over the place. That dodgy merchant was called something de Winter, and it's Dom's surname too."

Lola's eyes widened. "Are you sure?"

"One of the other kids definitely called him de Winter."

"So what was your de Winter saying, Lollie?" asked Reuben.

"That I can't tell you," she laughed. "I shared my house with five hungry brothers, remember. I was panicking I'd miss out on Gran's fajitas! I just remember glancing at the TV with my mouth full, and seeing those exact FX. And I remember my grandmother saying this guy was one scientist who actually cared about our planet's future."

"Did he?" asked Reuben.

Lola nodded vigorously. "He was definitely one of my century's good guys. Which is incredible considering the rest of his family."

"Don't get you," I said.

"Oh please," she said impatiently. "The de Winters have been creating mayhem since human history began. Of course, they don't always use that name," she added darkly.

"You make them sound like the PODS," I said.

Lola took a sip of her punch. "Trust me, the de Winters are like the PODS' special best friends on Earth. They're total gangsters. So when they got wind of this device, they went flat out to get the..." She frowned. "What's that thing which means an invention legally belongs to you?"

"The patent?" I suggested.

"Right, they wanted to get hold of the patent for themselves. There was this major court case. But finally the authorities ruled that the time device could lead to dangerous cosmic repercussions, so the court had it destroyed, plus all the relevant computer files were deleted."

"Yeah, but they weren't, were they!"

Our ice cubes tinkled madly as Reuben jumped up from the table.

His face blazed with excitement. "OK, maybe they destroyed the device, but someone obviously kept copies of the research."

Reuben's excitement was catching. "Omigosh," I gasped. "Someone's like, *reinvented* the device!"

"But however did those kids get hold of it?" breathed Lola.

"Good question," said Reuben. "But we'd better get down to the Agency ASAP and tell Michael."

But at that moment Amber appeared. "Sorry to interrupt, you guys," she said brightly. "Michael wants to see you. He says it's urgent!"

# CHAPTER SIX

"Maybe we should just move our beds down here," I complained as we flashed our IDs. "It would make things a whole lot simpler."

"This is my weirdest birthday ever," sighed Lola. "I never even got to open my present."

We jumped into the lift and went flashing up past various brilliantly lit floors with Lola still moaning on about her present. "Mo probably left it on the beach. I'll never get it now. Won't you just give me a tiny little clue what was inside?"

"No way," I told her.

We sped along the maze of gleaming corridors. Michael's door stood open. A blaze of diamond-white light poured out. This meant he had at least one archangel visitor.

Uh-oh, I thought. Not counting Michael, who is a total sweetie, I have this terrible mental block with archangels. I simply can't tell them apart. For one thing, they generate so much celestial radiance that apart from their eyes, it's hard to identify any actual features.

I squinted into the light and just made out two dazzling outlines.

"Er, hi!" I said shyly. "We got your message."

The light levels instantly grew more bearable, and Michael came sharply into focus. "Come in, come in!" he said warmly.

His visitor gave us a distant nod. Archangels aren't unfriendly exactly, it's more that they don't really do small talk.

We perched ourselves on uncomfortable office chairs, waiting for Michael to explain why we'd been summoned to the Agency for the second time that day. But his first words made my heart turn over.

"I just spoke to Orlando on the Link," he said.

I swallowed and said, "Oh, really?" about an octave higher than I intended. What *had* Orlando been telling him?

"As from tomorrow your Earth duties will change," Michael announced with a grave expression.

"Oh, right," I said bravely, picturing myself scrubbing a huge medieval lavvy with a very small toothbrush.

"Well, you were the only agents to witness the illicit time-travellers, which makes you the obvious choice for this mission."

I was stunned. "Orlando *told* you about them? But he said—"

Michael smiled. "He asked me to apologise for not giving you his full attention. When you reported the anomaly, he was having a rather sticky discussion with local personnel."

I was amazed. "So you actually believe us?"

"My dear child," sighed the mystery archangel. "Do you think we don't notice when humans go tinkering with cosmic laws?"

"As it happens, other agents detected similar anomalies." Michael checked his computer screen. "The latest was apparently in ancient Rome."

"That's right!" I turned excitedly to Lola. "Lollie, remember that girl saying the gladiators were lush?"

The archangel looked blank. "Lush?"

"It means really fit," I explained. "Presumably she was into big rippling muscles."

I could feel myself getting flustered and no wonder. I couldn't believe I was discussing sex with an archangel! Lola was trying desperately not to laugh.

Michael rescued us. "You may find these useful." He produced three pairs of sunglasses from a drawer and slid them across the desk.

"Oh, cool," I said.

The archangel sounded slightly tetchy. "These are not fashion accessories, Melanie. They are to help agents detect illicit emanations."

"Wow! How incredible," I breathed.

But I'm fairly sure Michael sussed I had no idea what his archangel colleague was on about, because he immediately explained about how each human energy system has to be specially customised, to fit his or her particular slot in time.

"Mr Allbright said something about that!" I said eagerly. "Except for geniuses, he said, who are like, ahead of their times."

"Correct," Michael agreed. "But even a genius has to share the same time band as her contemporaries. As you know, every time has different charms and challenges. Its own time 'weather' if you like. What you may not realise, is that this 'weather' leaves traces in the human energy field."

Lola perked up. "So these shades will help us to see auras, is that right?"

I was startled to hear Lola talking about auras as if they were like, a genuine scientific fact. I'd assumed they were invented by the same dodgy psychics who claim to get weird personal info from the dead.

"With practice you'll see energy emanations quite naturally," Michael explained. "But for the time being you'll probably find the glasses helpful."

Reuben seemed fascinated by his shades, tilting them back and forth, trying to figure out how they worked.

I cleared my throat. "Can I ask something?"

"Go ahead," said Michael.

"Well, humans have free will, right?"

He nodded. "That's correct."

"So why did the Agency ban time-travel? If humans have the brains to invent time-travel, why shouldn't they use it? If I'd had the chance to go time-travelling when I lived on Earth, I'd have gone like a shot, no question."

"'Banned' isn't quite the word I'd use," said Michael doubtfully. "But in more primitive eras, yes, time-travel is actively discouraged."

"But those kids didn't come from a primitive era," I objected. "They're from way in the future. They're almost, well, like angels."

"Mel's right," Lola chipped in. "It's like they're evolving into a new race or something."

"That's it exactly!" Michael sounded delighted that we'd figured this out for ourselves. "And one day, I promise you, humans will freely explore the fields of Time and Space. But not yet."

"Why not?" I argued. "I mean, Dom's just having a laugh. He's not doing anything like, *evil*."

"The child is playing with cosmic fire!" said a remote voice.

Archangels are incapable of losing their tempers. They're heaps too advanced. But his tone made me cringe.

"I don't think I understand," I said in a small voice.

He sighed. "Some humans will do anything for money. Sell fellow humans into slavery, rob the Earth of precious metals, poison the seas. For them Time is simply one more resource to pillage."

The archangel explained that humans could use the device to interfere with historical events, ensuring that certain people inherited lands or gold or oil wells.

"Not to mention scientific discoveries, priceless art treasures," Michael chipped in. "The list is endless..."

"I guess I wasn't thinking," I said humbly.

Reuben seemed doubtful. "What makes you think those kids will go back to medieval Marseilles anyway?"

Michael gave us one of his all-seeing smiles. "Let's just say I have a hunch."

I don't know about you, but I feel heaps more confident when I'm wearing the right clothes. So when I got back to the dorm, I forced myself to keep awake until I'd planned what I was going to wear next day. And like they say in the style magazines, that little bit of extra effort totally paid off. Because when my alarm went off all of two hours later, there was my trouble-shooting outfit all ready for me to jump into.

Actually my new look was pretty cool; Skechers trainers, boot-cut denim flares and a Triple 5 Soul hooded top in spicy orange. I quickly twisted the front of my hair into little Zulu knots, letting the rest cascade casually down my shoulders. Then I splashed on some Attitude, grabbed my tote bag and went to find Lola.

It was just getting light by the time we arrived back at the Agency, but I wasn't a bit tired. In fact I was buzzing with excitement.

Thanks to Orlando, we'd scored a cool new assignment detecting time misfits, and I was determined not to screw up. Here was my chance to prove I wasn't just some sad little airhead.

"Hey, Reubs," I said cheerfully, as we stepped into the time portal. "Was that Raphael or Japhiel in with Michael yesterday?"

Lola looked surprised. "Oh, I thought it was Gabriel."

"Uriel," said Reuben. "Definitely Uriel."

I giggled. "They should wear big gold initials on their chests like Superman."

Lola burst out laughing. "That is so wicked!"

But Reuben just said, "Who's Superman?"

And by the time we'd briefed our buddy on Earth's major superheroes, we were coming into land.

The instant we stepped on to solid ground, Lola and Reuben put on their Agency sunglasses. "Oh wow," they said simultaneously. "Mel, you've got to see this!"

So of course I put mine on too. "Oh wow," I breathed.

To think I'd walked around for thirteen years never knowing I had my own gorgeous wraparound rainbow.

I peered down at myself through my shades. "So where's mine?" I said disappointedly. "I mean angels must have massive auras, right?"

"The shades were invented to detect time anomalies," Reuben reminded me. "Not so vain little angels can play 'My energy field's bigger than your energy field'."

Lola laughed. "Ooooh! He really told you, Boo!"

We had a brilliant time, patrolling medieval Marseilles in our Agency shades going, "Oh wow, that one is totally luminous," and "Check that guy! Is his aura sinister or what!"

But after a while I noticed something disturbing. Everyone seemed to be talking about the same thing, a huge Crusader victory in the Holy Land. People were really over-excited, almost hysterical.

"Hey, there's Lucius!" said Lola. "Maybe he knows what's going on."

But there was no charming twinkle this morning. The Earth angel seemed deeply depressed. "The slavers start zis rumour deliberately," he sighed. "They think news of a crusader victory will make zese poor children even more desperate to board ze ships."

"Omigosh," I gasped. "Did it work?"

Lucius gave a shrug. "*Voilà.*"

I took off my shades and without any auras to distract me, immediately noticed what I'd failed to see earlier; kids practically climbing over each other to get to the little rowing boats bobbing alongside the jetty.

A boatman fended them off with an oar. "Go home! Forget about the crusades!" he yelled. "The ships are leaky as sieves. You will drown before you reach Jerusalem."

He obviously wanted to warn the kids off, but daren't name the slavers openly. But it was useless.

Hyped-up by the false rumours and terrified of missing their one chance of getting to the Holy Land, kids started diving off the dockside and swimming out towards the ships.

I caught sight of the older merchant, shaking his sleek silver hair, as if he didn't know what today's youngsters were coming to.

I was so upset that I put my shades back on without thinking. And then I saw them. Seven pulsating energy fields.

"Omigosh, they came back!" I shrieked. "Michael's right! Their auras are completely different!"

I whipped my glasses off again and the pulsing lights vanished.

In their place were Dom, his freckled friend and a new bunch of wide-eyed time tourists. "Isn't this cool?" I heard Dom say. "Isn't this worth every single penny?"

"So what do we do again?" asked a boy nervously.

Dom broke into an infectious grin. "Mingle with the natives of course! And try not to draw too much attention to yourself."

But it was too late for that. I saw the silver-haired merchant clock these new healthy specimens. And it was like, "Kerching!"

Then something really weird happened. Dom caught the merchant watching and I saw a flicker of horrified recognition in his eyes. He hastily pulled himself together. "Don't look round," he hissed. "Act like you've got somewhere to go and follow me!"

All seven kids sprinted down the nearest alleyway.

The merchant snapped his fingers. Four medieval heavies detached themselves from the crowd and went charging after them.

This was getting serious. "I'll watch the kids," I gabbled. "You guys get Orlando."

And I went hurtling after them.

This had to be the ultimate cosmic chase scene. Medieval heavies chasing illegal time-travellers, hotly pursued by an angel in Zulu knots!

The kids and I quickly put an impressive distance between ourselves and the thugs. Dom produced the time device, and breathlessly zapped its tiny keypads. The familiar time FX scribbles appeared. Dom waited with an agonised expression, counting to himself, as the luminous ropes became a twirling technicolour blur.

The thugs panted into view.

"NOW!" screamed Dom,

The kids dived simultaneously

I must have been a bit overexcited, because I didn't think twice. It seemed so obvious that I had to go after them. Behind me someone yelled, "Melanie, no!" But I totally ignored Orlando's warning. Taking a big breath, I jumped feet first into the future.

# CHAPTER SEVEN

I was in rushing darkness, lit by fierce stabs of lightning, and crackling with ancient sounds. Confused snatches of conversation, ferocious battle cries, muffled sobbing, long-lost love songs.

If I'd known Dom's device was so primitive, I'd never have risked it. Compared to that bone-rattling helter-skelter ride, angelic time-travel is a walk in the park.

At one point I was convinced I was turning inside out. That was just before all my limbs went dead. I couldn't actually tell if my body was still in one piece, or if I even had a body. I was totally numb.

And as I hurtled towards some unknown future century, deafening new sounds erupted around me. Explosions, wailing sirens, crazily mixed up with TV laughter and dog-food commercials and raw pounding hiphop. And I'd thought MY century was insane!

Then everything stopped, dead.

There was a silence so total I genuinely thought I'd gone deaf. Then I realised I could hear my own scared breathing in the dark. "Omigosh!" I whimpered. "Is it over?"

Had I been fast-forwarded to the end of the world by mistake? Had some hideous future war finally exterminated everyone on Earth? Was this the silence of total nothingness?

Actually, no. Because all at once I heard something. The tiny liquid sound of a bird singing. A bird and a soft whisper of wind through leaves and somewhere in the distance, a small child laughing its socks off.

I felt my eyes fill with tears. The human race had pulled through! This wasn't an ominous hush. It was world peace, how about that!

And suddenly all the feeling flooded back into my body. It was agony, the worst pins and needles ever. And with a terrifying whoosh, I landed on solid ground. Seconds later, Reuben and Lola crashed down on top of me.

"OW!! What are you doing here, you morons?" I hissed.

"You didn't think we'd let you swan off to the future on your own!" Reuben gasped out.

Lola just lay whimpering softly. "Tell me we don't have to do that again," she moaned.

We lay in a tangled heap, trying to get our breath back.

It was almost evening and I could smell a sweet fresh smell, like the smell you get in really expensive flower shops. We'd crash-landed in someone's old summerhouse. From where I was lying, I could see bright blue trumpet-shaped flowers and a glossy orange tree complete with perfect baby oranges. I felt pangs of jealousy. I've got a v. small orange tree in my room. I grew it in ten minutes flat, when I helped in Miss Dove's nursery class one time. But though I water it faithfully every day, it still hasn't produced a single orange.

I dimly registered Dom's school mates melting out of sight between some pillars. I knew we should follow them, but I couldn't seem to move. Then Lola gave a tiny gasp, so naturally I looked up. Staring down at us with stunned expressions were Dom and his little freckled girlfriend.

I was so shocked that I actually stopped breathing. We were visible!

The device must have messed up our angel molecules, causing us to materialise.

The girl pulled off her medieval head dress and all this frizzy red hair sprang out. With her looks she could totally have gone on as orphan Annie without a rehearsal. (If it wasn't for the scowl, obviously.) She jerked her thumb in our direction. "What are they?"

"I have no idea," Dom admitted. "But if a teacher sees them, we're history."

I almost shrieked with laughter. I know it's not cool for an angel to have hysterics. But I was in shock. Thanks to me, my angel buddies were totally exposed to human view, and I had no idea what to do.

Then I heard the creak of the summerhouse door and the sound of approaching footsteps. "Dom, Lily! Do I have to come and get you?" said a friendly voice.

Dom froze. "It's Mr Lamb."

Lily looked appalled. "Oh no! We totally forgot about Metaphysics."

They started frantically changing into their normal clothes, not space suits with slanting zips as you might think, but the twenty-third century equivalent of smart casuals.

"Is metaphysics like metalwork?" I whispered.

"More like philosophy," Reuben whispered back.

Ooer, I thought. Talk about high fliers.

"I tried to tell you," Lily was moaning. "Twice in two days is pushing it, I said. Someone's going to rumble us, I said, but oh no—"

"Will you just shut up, Lil! No-one's going to rumble anyone. Let me do the talking, OK?"

"Yeah, and how d'you plan to explain the time stowaways?"

*Time stowaways?* I sagged with relief. They obviously had no idea that we were angels.

Leaves rustled madly. "I know you're in here!" the teacher called. Any minute now he was going to find our hiding place.

Lola smiled at the kids. "Don't worry," she said in perfect future slang. "We won't grass. Just tell us what you want us to say."

Dom looked panic-stricken. "Don't say anything," he pleaded. "You have no idea what you're getting into."

All the tiny oranges trembled on their stalks as a man came pushing through the foliage. He had one of those bland harmless faces, like a kids' TV presenter. "There you are! Everyone's waiting."

I saw the teacher suppress his surprise. "And who's this?" he said in a joky voice.

"It's OK, Mr Lamb, I can explain—" Dom began.

"Don't worry, we're just leaving!" I interrupted airily. "Our parents are thinking of sending us to your brilliant school, so Dom and Lily kindly offered to show us round." I dug Reuben in the ribs.

"Oh, yeah," he said solemnly. "Great school."

"Wow, is that the time!" said Lola. "We'd better get moving."

But somehow nice harmless Mr Lamb had got between us and the door. "Sorry kids," he said in his child-friendly voice. "You know the rules. No-one enters or leaves a Phoenix School unless we've checked your ID. You'll have to come with me."

I saw genuine terror flicker across Dom's face. What could possibly be scaring him so badly? I wondered. We obediently trailed after the teacher.

Lola pulled a face at me. "I feel totally naked."

"You feel naked," Reuben muttered. "I've got major stage fright. I can't believe humans can actually *see* me!"

I wondered if materialising without permission was still a cosmic offence, if you did it by mistake. I mean, we hadn't actually blown our divine cover or anything.

Then we went through the door into the school grounds, and everything else went clean out of my head as Lola went, "Ohhh."

The sun was setting, bathing everything in its warm peachy light. Kids in stylish casuals flitted about the campus, chatting, laughing and generally being kids.

Lovely music drifted from windows. Several pupils were practising martial arts under the trees. Every child had that special glow I'd noticed in Dom and his mates.

I think Reuben had forgotten about his stage fright because his eyes shone with excitement. "Lollie's right! These humans are *way* more evolved. They've totally grown out of that primitive war stage. Now they're producing beautiful genius kids. It's literally Heaven on Earth!"

It all sounded so tempting, and you have *no* idea how much I wanted to believe him. But like Mr Allbright says, we should always listen to our angel intuition, and mine just wasn't convinced. Look closer, Mel, it insisted. What's wrong with this picture?

Take the teacher. He knew what Dom had been up to, I was sure of it. OK, he hadn't actually sussed we were angels, but he'd definitely twigged we weren't from their time-zone. So why was he stringing us along, as if he'd genuinely swallowed our story?

Mr Lamb took us into a building so perfect that I could not believe it was a school. There was the sweetest indoor garden with a little Zen fountain and shells and coloured gravel, plus they'd hung the kids' artwork everywhere, not Blutacked any old how, but beautifully framed, as if the teachers actually valued it. The school even *smelled* lovely.

I was wrong about this place, I thought dreamily. This really is Heaven on Earth.

Then I saw the retina scanner and my heart dropped into my trainers. As you probably guessed, we don't do retina scans in Heaven.

We had to take turns to stand in front of the machine, trying not to blink, while eerie blue lights sizzled and flashed, like those evil flykiller thingies they have in chip shops.

Not surprisingly the scan showed that my mates and I had no official existence in the twenty-third century.

The teacher vanished into an office and I heard him talking softly on the phone. "Definitely not from this era. Of course. Yes, I'll hold on to them until the authorities get here."

And like a tiny candle flame, my vision of a peaceful harmonious future gave a last sad little flicker and blew out.

Mr Lamb reappeared. "Sorry about this kids," he said in his jolly TV presenter voice. "But until we sort out this little mix-up, we'll have to keep you here, I'm afraid."

He wagged his finger at Dom and Lily. "And you two have a class to go to!"

Dom looked desperately strained. "Bye, you guys," he said feebly.

But the Mr Nice Guy act was obviously for Dom and Lily's benefit, because the minute the kids disappeared, he hustled us upstairs and shoved us into an empty classroom. "I don't know who you are," he snapped. "But believe me, I'm going to find out!" And his tone was pure menace.

The door slammed and I heard an ominous clunk as he locked us in.

I looked miserably around the room. With its pastel pink walls and teeny tiny furniture it looked almost exactly like Miss Dove's angel nursery class. But somehow that only made our situation more depressing.

"Still think it's Heaven on Earth?" I said in a sour voice.

"Sorry," Reuben said humbly. "I got a bit starry-eyed, didn't I."

He looked so forlorn that I felt really ashamed of myself.

"It's OK, Reubs," I said quickly. "You'll get the hang of it."

"Yeah, don't beat yourself up, Sweetpea," said Lola. "I lived on this gorgeous planet for thirteen years and I have NO idea what's going on at this school."

"Me neither," I admitted. "It looks perfect. But something's just that little bit off."

"Totally," said Reuben. "But what? None of this makes sense."

Lola sighed. "It looks like the cosmic musketeers are seriously out of their depth this time."

"We'd better call up the Agency," said Reuben gloomily. "Get them to beam us home."

We fished out our angel tags, centred ourselves and tried to connect with the Link. We waited patiently. But nothing happened. No cosmic tingles. No answering heavenly vibe. Nothing.

"I hate to depress you," said Reuben, "but I think that device demagnetised our tags."

My stomach gave a lurch. "You're kidding!"

Lola sounded scared. "But we can still get out of here? We can still dematerialise?"

"Sure we can," I said bravely. "We're angels, right?"

But a quarter of an hour later, we were still 100% visible.

I slumped on to a tiny chair. This nightmare was all my fault.

At the Academy, our teachers are constantly telling us we shouldn't try to be heroes. But had I listened? No, as usual I'd just gone ahead and done my own sweet thing without once thinking of the consequences.

I could tell that Lola was trying to keep calm. She wandered around the classroom, inspecting the work on the walls. "Hey, these babies are doing really cool stuff."

Reuben started doing martial-art stretching exercises. He said it helped him to think. "What did that guy call this school again?" he called over his shoulder.

I wasn't in the mood for giving Earth lessons to be honest. "A Phoenix School," I said wearily. "A phoenix is a mythical bird. When it's old and ready to die, it sets fire to its nest, and a little baby phoenix chick is reborn from the ashes—"

He instantly straightened up. "That's so beautiful!" he breathed. "It's like these genius schools are the new hope born from the destruction of the past."

"Pity about their teacher training," Lola said sarcastically.

"We only met one teacher," Reuben pointed out. "The others might be total saints."

"So why are we getting these weird vibes—" I began.

But just then we heard something scrape against the window.

A ladder appeared. Its top rungs waved about wildly, then came to rest against the glass.

Voices drifted up from below. "They came out of nowhere!" Dom was explaining excitedly, and Lily grumbled something I couldn't catch. "I told you, I'll sort it," said a male voice.

I stiffened. I'd heard that voice before.

The ladder grated against the glass as someone started climbing up. "You'll have to open it from inside," called the voice.

I felt myself go dizzy. *It can't be.*

It was like a bad dream. I tried to scream a warning, but my vocal cords were paralysed. I couldn't even move, just watched helplessly as Reuben ran to flip the catch.

The glass slid back and a boy appeared outside the window.

His eyes were as beautiful as I remembered. Beautiful and totally empty. "Hi, Melanie, how's it going?" he said smoothly.

It was Brice.

## CHAPTER EIGHT

Reuben instantly went into a defensive martial-arts stance, but Brice totally didn't take any notice. He jumped down into the room, his face carefully blank like a gymnast bringing off a tricky dismount.

"The ladder seems OK, so you shouldn't have any problems," he said. "I'm not saying it's great or anything. It's probably better not to make any sudden moves."

Apart from his twenty-third century casuals, my deadly enemy looked just the same, the exact double of a boy I once had this hopeless crush on. The PODS adore having this kind of humiliating info about people. It gives them a major power rush.

I realised he was avoiding my eyes. In fact if it

was anyone but Brice I'd have said he was nervous, rabbiting on like he was our special best friend.

"Hope you don't mind heights, Sanchez," he said.

"I'm an angel, moron," Lola snapped. "Air is my natural element."

"How are you with heights incidentally?" I asked sarkily. "Now that you're a – oh, what is the correct term for a fallen angel these days?" I asked my mates. "A former angel? An ex-angel?"

For the first time I saw a flash of the old Brice. "Cut this angel garbage," he snarled. "Just climb down the ladder and get out of my life."

No-one moved. It wasn't that we were defying him, more that this whole situation was too weird. None of us knew how to handle it.

He flung up his hands. "Fine! Stay here! But I don't think you're going to like what happens next. Future science labs, weird tests."

Lola looked disgusted. "Oh, please! Like you'd actually care. I can't believe you're daring to show your face after what you did."

"Yeah, why would you help us?" I said disbelievingly.

He gave his cold laugh. "I don't give a monkey's about you, darling. It's Dom I care about."

"Yeah right!" I snorted. The idea of Brice caring for someone was just bizarre.

"Will you guys just get a move on?" Dom called hoarsely.

To my astonishment Reuben shrugged. "Well, we obviously can't stay here. I say we take a chance."

Lola was scandalised. "Are you nuts? How do we know he hasn't got some gruesome little PODS posse down there?"

Brice gave her a nasty grin. "I guess you'll just have to trust me!"

But when we reached the ground, we only found Dom and Lily waiting. Dom was still agitated about something. I heard him whispering to Brice.

"I'll look after it, mate, if you're worried," Brice offered.

Omigosh, I thought. Things were getting worse by the second. My mates and I gave each other helpless glances, as Dom handed the time device to our cosmic enemy.

"Now let's see if you can keep the school rules till bedtime, eh Dom?" Brice gave Dom's arm an affectionate biff.

"Dave's always getting me out of trouble," Dom explained bashfully. "He's like my guardian angel."

There was a stunned silence.

Reuben recovered first. "That's erm, great," he said a little too brightly "Everyone needs a guardian angel. Right, *Dave*?"

"Right," said Brice, looking incredibly uncomfortable.

When Dom and Lily had gone, Brice let out a sigh of relief. "It's cool. He has no idea who you are."

"He certainly doesn't know who *you* are!" I snorted. "So what's a bright kid like Dom doing mixed up with a jerk like you?"

Lola's lip curled. "Maybe Brice is like, grooming him to be his evil successor."

The air practically crackled with tension. I genuinely thought Brice was going to hit her. Reuben quickly put himself between them.

Brice was so furious he could hardly get the words out. "You kids are all so freaking morally superior! Even when you have *no* idea what you're talking about."

She shrugged. "Oh, please, put us right, *hombre*. We're hanging on your every word."

"It will be my pleasure," he spat.

We didn't exactly have a choice. Normally nothing would induce us to hang out with Brice. But as you know, he had the time device, so where he went, we had to follow.

He led us through the beautifully kept grounds to one of the dorms. A little kid spotted us. "Hey who are you?" he yelled.

"Oh, we're ange—" Reuben began eagerly.

"Shut up!" Brice shoved him roughly through the door.

We followed him up a flight of stairs to a large open-plan kitchen. It was a really homey space with sofas and a massive blackboard. I suppose that was in case a young genius felt the need to solve a mathematical equation while he was heating his baked beans.

Someone was practicing a cello in one of the upstairs rooms. It sounded beautiful yet tragic, you know how they do. All at once I felt horribly depressed. It had just dawned on me that I had screwed up a major celestial mission.

I found myself compulsively listing my latest cosmic boo-boos, and there were quite a few. Materialising without permission, stranding my mates in the distant future, damaging Agency property (our platinum tags); damaging them so badly in fact, that we couldn't even let the Agency know where we were.

Worst of all, we'd just watched like lemons as Dom handed a dangerous time device to the PODS' favourite messenger boy.

Miss Rowntree was right, I thought bleakly. I'm just an airhead with attitude.

I didn't know what else to do, so I went to gaze out of the window.

A set of tail-lights were moving slowly along a tree-lined avenue. In the distance I could see a gorgeous house, ghostly pale in the twilight. The kind of house I'd once dreamed of buying my mum, when I was rich and famous. Though of course, as it turned out, I didn't live long enough to be either.

A jeering voice cut through my thoughts. "Well, kiddiwinks, are you ready to be shocked out of your tiny angel minds?"

I could see Brice's reflection in the glass. He was doing his cosmic outlaw pose; thumbs in belt-loops, mean expression.

A terrible tiredness came over me. "You can always try," I said wearily.

"Then sit down," he said. "This could take a while."

And Brice started to tell us a story so horrifying, that it might almost be true.

## Chapter Nine

"Once upon a time I was a human being." Brice sounded coldly chatty, like nothing he was saying actually mattered. "And sorry, Mel, I didn't live in the distant past, as you'd like to believe."

"You lived in this century, didn't you?" said Reuben softly.

"Correct, angel boy. This was my little personal slot in time. This school was also my school. And Dominic de Winter, amateur time-tours operator – well, he was my little brother."

I think I actually gasped. But Brice was still talking.

"Dom was just three when I died. And before you ask, he has no idea we're related. He doesn't remember he even had a brother. A little magic trick of mine."

I was horrified. "Didn't your parents tell him?"

Brice's eyes glittered. "Dad was out of the picture by this time. As for Mum, well, better not get me started on her."

The cello was still sobbing away overhead and frankly I wished whoever was playing would just knock it off. Things were already tense enough.

Brice took a breath. "Everyone uses that word 'family', like we're all talking about the same thing. But my family is truly unique. Oh, on the surface, we're incredibly civilised, darlings. But underneath – oh man, it's like swimming with crocodiles."

He laughed. "Yeah, crocodiles is about right. In the days before war was banned, you'd always find a de Winter lurking at the bottom of the pond, making a stonking profit. No matter which country lost or won, the de Winters made a killing. They'd buy and sell anything. Guns, bombs, planes, medicines, artificial limbs, human beings..."

Brice watched dreamily as several sets of tail-lights went glimmering slowly up the avenue towards the house. I counted five – no, six vehicles. They must be having a party, I thought vaguely.

"Isn't it funny how each kid always thinks he'll be different?" Brice said. "They see their parents screw up and they say, 'Uh-uh, not me! I'm better than that. I'm going to change the world.'"

"Some of them do," Lola pointed out.

"Oh spare me," he said. "Aren't you guys ever off duty?"

Lola's eyes were steely. "I don't know. Are you?"

"Just let the guy talk," Reuben told her.

Brice was still watching the cars. "But Dom really was different," he said softly. "I saw that right from the start. The kind of kid Phoenix schools were invented for. Bright, sensitive, totally magic."

The cello stopped abruptly. A door banged overhead and a small boy came flying down the stairs, lugging an instrument case practically twice his size.

Brice waited until the baby cellist was out of earshot.

"Don't laugh, but when Dom was born, I actually thought I was getting a chance to make up for all the bad stuff I'd done. I made this ridiculous promise to myself. I was going to save my little baby bro from our evil reptile rellies." Brice laughed. "But like I said, I died.

"But here's the really hilarious part, you guys. It turned out I'd been talent-spotted by someone at the Agency who decided I'd make an absolutely super angel!"

He blew out his breath. "Woo! Talk about culture shock! No blackmail, no lies, no undercover thuggery. Just never-ending bliss."

Brice's voice grew softly intimate. "It feels so safe in the Heavenly City, doesn't it, Mel? Like nothing could ever hurt you?"

I felt my skin begin to creep. I hated the thought of Brice going anywhere near my favourite heavenly hang-outs.

He was talking as if it was just the two of us alone together. "At nights I'd lie in my narrow little bed in the Academy dorm, listening to that cosmic lullaby you like so much, Melanie. The humming-top music?"

I went bright red. Brice loves to make out that he has this private window into my mind.

"It's OK, sweetheart," he jeered. "Your lullaby never did it for me. I was far too worried imagining what my family was doing to Dom."

He started pacing. "Oh, Michael gave me all the usual guff about how no-one's ever really alone on Earth. And I'm thinking, well I was on Earth for fifteen freaking years and you never helped me. And I'm supposed to trust you with my baby brother!"

He was back at the window now, staring out at the house. "Anyway, why would the Agency help a de Winter kid, a bad seed? It didn't make sense."

Something about Brice's life story must have really got under my skin, because to my annoyance my eyes went all blurry with tears.

Will you get a grip, Melanie, I snuffled to myself. You're supposed to be thinking up a plan to get the time device away from this creep, not sympathising with his lousy childhood.

Luckily my soul-mate is made of sterner stuff. "OK, we've heard your tragic story," she said in a bored voice. "What's your point?"

Brice whirled round. "What's my *point*! To educate you, Sanchez. I'm giving you brats a free reality lesson."

"Yeah, right," Lola snorted. "Like you're the only person who ever suffered."

"Stop it," said Reuben. "Stop it right now. Can't you see this is just what they want?"

Our angel buddy didn't even raise his voice, yet it went right through me like a bell. Everyone shut up, even Brice.

"Better," said Reuben calmly, and he nodded towards the window. "Now Brice can tell us what's going on up at the house."

"Oh, that," Brice said in a careless voice. "My evil rellies are having a get-together."

"Like a party, you mean?" I said.

"You have no idea how big my family is, have you? No, I'm not boasting, Sanchez," he added, seeing Lola's scathing expression. "I'm trying to explain that this is not some small local nightmare you've stumbled into. Oh, no. It's global, baby. The cars you saw just now? They're just the latecomers. Guests have been arriving from all over the world for days."

"OK, so your family has flash parties," Lola began but he totally ignored her.

"That house with its oh-so-distressing vibes belongs to my uncle, Jonas de Winter. Didn't you realise? He's the Phoenix school headmaster."

My mouth completely turned to cotton wool. *What's wrong with this picture*, I'd asked. Now I knew.

Omigosh, I thought. It wasn't the school which was radiating confusing signals. It was my lovely dream house.

Brice gave a terrible laugh. "You've got to hand it to the de Winters. We're adaptable. War is out. Peace is in. Hey, let's take over a Phoenix school and use it as cover for our less respectable activities."

Lola frowned. "So why the party?"

He looked surprised. "To celebrate Dom's achievement, of course."

"Huh?" Lola and I stared at him.

"Oh, do try to keep up, you guys!" said Reuben impatiently. "Dom reinvented the time device. Didn't you figure that out yet?"

I stared at him. "But he's just a kid."

"A Phoenix kid," he said. "A boy genius."

It seemed that de Winter scientists had been trying to reconstruct the device for decades. Finally they were almost there, but there was one tiny detail they simply couldn't figure out.

Then Dom won a major science prize and the Family were over the moon. Maybe little Dom could succeed where the scientists had failed. Someone "accidentally" left the relevant research material at Dom's mum's place, where he was bound to find it in the holidays. Then they sat back and waited. They didn't have to wait long.

"Dom knocks a prototype together in like, a weekend, but my little brother is this total innocent. He has absolutely *no* idea what he's got himself into! So what does he do with this world-shattering invention?" Brice looked as if he didn't know whether to laugh or cry.

"He runs a time-tour scam for his mates?" I suggested.

Brice made an impatient gesture. "The little idiot could have got himself killed, but do you think Mum and the rest of them care? No, they just want to know if the thing actually works. So they simply look the other way and *let* him take all these stupid risks."

"Can't someone stop them?" I asked.

"No-one stops the de Winters, believe me. Oh, sure they're human. Just. If you stick pins in them, they bleed. When their hearts stop, they snuff it. But there's always another de Winter to take their place."

"But the government—" I objected feebly.

He shook his head. "The government has no idea they're there. The de Winters are masters at camouflaging their activities. It's an art form, how they operate. They suck people in so gradually they don't even notice it happening. A well-timed reward here, a little painful pressure there, until they own you body and soul."

"They'll never own Dom," I said fiercely.

"They'll never own Dom," he mimicked. 'Don't make me laugh. They'd have got him years ago, if it wasn't for me."

"So how come you were allowed back to these times to keep an eye on your brother?" said Reuben.

There was an electric pause, then Brice said lightly, "Oh, the er, usual deal."

"You made a deal with the Agency?" I was shocked.

Lola shook her head. "He sold his soul, Boo. To the PODS."

Brice shrugged. "You know the great thing about the Dark Powers. They keep things simple. They don't give a monkey's about your morals or motives. It's a straightforward trade. I do them favours. They let me keep an eye on Dom."

"Now tell us the bad thing about the PODS," Reuben said softly.

The question seemed to take Brice by surprise. I saw a tiny muscle move in his cheek. "I told you, they're cool. Anyway, I'm a big boy. I can handle it."

We just waited. Eventually he said, "The worst thing is when they won't let me see Dom. Last time they didn't let me near him for months. You saw what he got up to then."

"That's when he re-invented the time device, right?" I said.

"Do you blame him?" said Brice angrily. "He was in our mother's house for a whole summer. He was lonely as hell."

"How do we know this isn't one of your sick little games?" Lola said suddenly. "Like, 'Oh I'll make the angels believe my sad story, then catch them off-guard and totally trash them'."

"I don't really care what you think, darling," drawled Brice. "I know why I'm here, that's all that matters."

Reuben's voice was quiet. "I believe him."

Lola was horrified. "After what he did to you in London!"

"Like I said," he repeated firmly, "I believe him."

Sometimes pure angels take your breath away. After all Brice had done to him, our buddy was still willing to give him another chance.

But the weird thing is, I thought Reuben was right.

For the first time Brice made a warped kind of sense. He wasn't just some evil cosmic joker delighting in chaos. He actually loved someone. He loved his brother like I loved my sister Jade. But unlike me, he didn't trust anyone else to keep his brother safe.

Brice only trusted one person. Brice.

The atmosphere in the room had totally morphed. I think even Lola was on the verge of giving our old enemy the benefit of the doubt. And perhaps our expressions had changed or something, because Brice's face suddenly shut like a trap.

"OK, the freak show's over. Now flutter off back to Heaven where everything is pretty and nothing hurts."

"But I thought you—" My voice trailed off.

"You thought I wanted your help!" Brice's face twisted. "Don't make me laugh! I've taken care of Dom all his life and I don't need a bunch of little angels getting in my hair. You've got him into enough trouble as it is. So just shove off."

A door slammed and a desperate voice yelled, "Dave? Dave, are you there?"

Dave? I thought dimly. Who's he? Then I remembered that bad-boy Brice was currently posing as good-guy Dave.

Lily came charging upstairs. She'd gone so white that all her freckles were standing out like braille. She could hardly get the words out for crying. "I'm so scared," she gasped at last. "They've got Dom."

Brice looked as if he might be sick with shock. "What do you mean?"

"They know what he's been up to..." Lily babbled.

I knew instantly who she meant by "they". The de Winters.

"... about the device and everything. They said he had to hand it over. Dom said he had no idea what they were on about. I totally lost it, Dave. I said I saw him give it to you, so they sent me to find you. I've been looking everywhere!"

In other circumstances I'd have been sorry for her, but I'd gone completely cold inside. I backed away from Brice in horror. We'd been such *idiots*. Brice didn't love Dom. He didn't give a stuff about anyone and he never had. He'd been working for the PODS all along.

"You evil jerk!" I was in tears of fury. "I can't believe even you would stoop so low. You actually betrayed your own brother!"

# CHAPTER TEN

To my astonishment, Brice just stood there, taking all my contempt and hatred like he thought he totally deserved it. It was weirdly dignified somehow, and I have to admit it kind of took the wind out of my sails.

He waited until I'd finally run out of abuse, then said, "Go back to the house, Lily. Tell them I'll bring the device."

"You hate me, don't you?" she said miserably. "I don't blame you. I really hate myself. But they said they'd hurt him and they meant it too. I've never seen Mr de Winter like that before. He always seemed so—"

"You don't need to explain, believe me," Brice interrupted. "You did the right thing. Now run back to Mr de Winter, and give him my message, OK?"

But Lily hovered, looking anxious. "Dave," she blurted out, "why did she say you were Dom's brother?"

"Oh, Mel's just a bit confused," Brice said smoothly. "Time-travel scrambles people's brain cells sometimes."

I glowered at him. But Lily seemed reassured by this explanation. She rushed downstairs and a few seconds later I saw a little figure go racing through the dusk.

"You can't do this, Brice," said Reuben in a low voice. "These people have been feeding off human misery for centuries."

I clenched my fists. "Yeah, and now he's going to hand them history on a plate, so they can rip off everyone they missed first time around."

"You don't know that for certain," Lola said softly.

I shot her a betrayed look. I couldn't believe she was standing up for Brice. I was *so* upset. It wasn't just Brice. It was everything.

I remembered how I'd felt when I heard the bird singing outside the summerhouse. Humans had so nearly got their act together, but they just had to mess it up, didn't they?

I mean, what's the use of creating Heaven on Earth, if you don't take proper care of it? What's the use of schools for genius kids, if you let an evil family like the de Winters exploit them for their own sinister ends? They didn't ban war at all, I thought miserably. The suffering is still going on. Like Brice said, it's just out of sight.

I buried my face in my hands.

Brice's voice was unusually tender. "You're wrong about me, Mel," he said. "I might be a jerk and a creep, but I'd never betray Dominic. I'm trying to save him, and I will. He's got something they want, something they'll do anything to get, even if it means letting Dom leave the Family."

"You're crazy," I said in a muffled voice. "These guys bamboozle whole governments. They're not exactly going to play fair with a kid."

"They will. If you help me," he said hesitantly.

"Erm, excuse me," objected Lola. "'Buzz off,' you said. 'I can take care of Dom by myself,' you said. 'You angel brats are so freaking superior,' you said."

Brice rolled his eyes. "Give me a break, Sanchez. I can't be seen in that house. They'll know who I am."

"How come?" I said.

"My mum's there, isn't she? She may not be the best mum in the world but even she'd recognise her deceased eldest son."

I stared at him. "You mean that's your *real* face?" The words were out before I could stop them and I felt my face burn with embarrassment.

I'd naturally assumed that Brice had disguised himself as my bad-boy crush, purely to humiliate me. It never occurred to me this was how he actually *looked* in his lifetime.

Suddenly Brice grabbed my arm. His energy felt weird, kind of comfortingly familiar and terrifyingly alien all at the same time. His eyes blazed. "Say you'll help me?"

"Hey," said Lola angrily. "Let her go, creep!"

I felt Brice press something into my hand. "Mel, your job is to look after humans, not save history," he said. "History's just an idea. My brother's real."

And he'd gone.

I uncurled my fingers and found a wafer-thin piece of plastic, about the size of a regular KitKat. Brice had given me the time device.

We looked at each other helplessly. I'm pretty sure we were all thinking the same thing. If we'd been human, all our troubles would be over. Unfortunately we were angels on a cosmic mission.

"I can't *believe* he did that," Lola wailed. "That was so sneaky. It's our one chance to get back home, and he knows we can't use it."

For once, I disagreed with Lola. I had the feeling Brice had acted completely spontaneously. It was like he'd trusted us to do the right thing.

"So now what?" said Lola.

Reuben gave her a serene smile. "I guess we do what he says."

Lola looked appalled. "Give the device to the evil de Winters! Are you crazy!"

A strange calm flowed into me, a welcome sign that my angel intuition had totally kicked in. "He's right," I said. "Come on guys, we're going to a party!"

We crept down the drive to the headmaster's house, carefully keeping in the shadows.

But as we got closer to the house, a terrible tiredness came over me. Like, what *is* the point. There was no way we could do this alone – and no matter what anyone said, we were *totally* alone. With our tags out of action, we couldn't even call home for back-up. If the Agency really cared about us, they wouldn't put us through this, I thought miserably. It's simply too much responsibility. We're just kids. We're not even properly trained yet.

By this time, it was an effort just to keep walking. It felt as if I had invisible stones in my pockets weighing me down.

Suddenly Lola whispered, "Anyone else getting a PODS vibe?"

Reuben pulled a face. "Just a bit."

Lola gave a low chuckle. "Phew! What a relief! Thought I was having a major crack-up there for a while!"

Honestly, what would you do without your mates? My depression vanished like magic.

"I'm so embarrassed," I hissed. "I can't believe I fell for that old doom 'n despair routine!"

"Me neither. I suppose we should have expected it," whispered Lola. "The de Winters might be human, but they've been in cahoots with the PODS since history began. This place must be saturated with evil vibes."

"It is. You can feel it." Reuben tapped his solar plexus. "But it's so pretty, you think you're imagining it."

We had almost reached the house. The atmosphere was incredibly foul. Lola said it was like wading through evil cosmic treacle, but frankly I don't think there are any words to describe it. Normally in a situation like this, we'd use our tags to access extra angelic protection through the Link. Unfortunately this was not an option.

The house was ablaze with light. No-one had drawn the curtains, so we could see right into the downstairs rooms. It was the most luxurious place I have ever seen, like a celebrity's house from a twenty-third century *Hello!*.

We slipped through a side entrance and crept stealthily up a velvety carpeted corridor. I heard soft chinks of crockery and a subdued murmur of voices.

Passing an open door, I saw staff in uniforms bustling around a vast dining room, smoothing crisp tablecloths, buffing up silver and twitching at gorgeous flower arrangements, making everything perfect for the big party.

It was all so beautiful, yet I just wanted to bolt out of that house and never come back.

My mates obviously felt the same way, because at the same moment they grabbed hold of my hands.

"Oh that is *so* touching," said a mocking voice in my ear. "Excuse me while I puke."

Brice hadn't gone away after all. He'd just made himself invisible.

"Are you trying to give me heart failure?" I snapped. "What are you doing here, anyway?"

"You don't seriously think I'd trust my brother to a bunch of little halo polishers?" Brice inquired.

I was completely confused. "But you said your family would see you."

"Get a grip, Melanie. I said I couldn't let myself be *seen*. Hey, my people might run with the PODS, but they don't interact with the dead, sweetheart."

"So if you're here, why do you need us?" hissed Lola.

"I told you, Sanchez. We're going to save Dom. My way."

You can't exactly glare at someone who's invisible, so I had to resort to sarcasm. "You ooze charm, don't you," I said in disgust.

"Oh, he definitely oozes," said Lola. "But charm? I don't think so."

"Will you just give the guy a break?" sighed Reuben.

"Hey, buddy, I can stand up for myself, you know!" objected Brice's disembodied voice.

This was definitely the weirdest situation of my short angel career.

OK, so I still haven't quite finished reading *The Angel Handbook*, but I'll bet good money it doesn't say anything about the forces of light actively like, co-operating with the forces of darkness! But what choice did we have?

Exactly!

So following Brice's whispered directions, we found our way to the foot of a seriously majestic staircase. It was just like the ones people dance down in old musicals and my mum would have totally adored it.

Crouching on the bottom stair, looking more like orphan Annie than ever, was Lily. She sprang up in a panic. "Where's Dave?"

"He got held up," I said hastily. "Don't worry, we've got the device."

Poor Lily almost fainted with relief.

We followed her up the stairs.

As we reached the first floor, some beautifully dressed little kids went scampering happily across the landing and out of sight.

Peals of laughter came from one of the rooms. I could hear a hum of cultured voices as the international de Winters made small talk in all the major European languages.

Brice prodded me unpleasantly in the ribs.

"Hey, no physical contact, OK?" I hissed.

"Stop being coy, darling, and look through that door," he hissed back. "There's someone I want you to see."

A woman sat with her back to us. I could see her upswept hair, long suntanned legs and an elegant hand gesturing as she talked. Wafts of expensive perfume drifted my way.

She looked amazingly stylish, yet even without my agency shades, I knew there was something alarmingly wrong with this woman's energy field. She's like this house, I thought. Lovely to look at. Totally deadly inside.

Brice sounded amused. "That's Laura de Winter," he said. "She's my mother."

I had the horrible feeling he'd just read my mind. "Oh," I said, "She's erm, really…"

"Toxic?" he suggested. "Dad certainly thought so."

"Oh yeah, and what was he like?" I burbled, desperately trying to cover my embarrassment.

"I have no idea. I hardly knew him. He was a scientist. A brilliant one apparently. The Family hired him to solve the time-device problem. They wanted to keep him keen, so they married him to Mum."

"You're kidding," I breathed.

"Time goes by, Dad earns the Family's trust, blah blah blah. They leak vital info about their dodgier activities. Dad doesn't like what he hears and unwisely makes no attempt to hide his feelings. The de Winters decide he's failed the Family loyalty test, so obviously he has to go."

I gasped. "They *killed* him?"

"Good as. They faked a big scandal and Dad mysteriously disappeared. It happened just before I died. Dom doesn't know a thing about it."

"Well, I think your dad sounds great," I said. "He totally stood up for his principles."

"And a lot of good it did him," Brice said bitterly.

I started spinning romantic fantasies of reuniting Dom with his scientist dad. "Do you know where he is?" I asked.

"Will you just drop it?" Brice snapped. "The guy's a loser. He works nights in some freaking laundry or something. Only the evil survive, haven't you figured that out by now?"

I felt a flicker of pity. So that's why Brice has such a warped attitude, I thought. He's scared to join the good guys, in case he ends up like his dad.

I saw my mates waiting at the end of the corridor and hurried to catch them up.

"Where did you get to?" Reuben complained.

"She's fraternising with the enemy," said Brice.

"You wish," I told him under my breath.

Lily was tapping at an ornate panelled door.

A cultured voice called, "Come!"

We followed Lily into an imposing boardroom.

I vaguely noticed drapy curtains with ties of floppy gold rope, and a long table of dark wood, polished so brightly it looked exactly like glass. Around it sat maybe fifteen or twenty people, presumably key members of the de Winter family.

They were all of different ages and races, but their hungry expressions were identical. Like they were just about to get what they wanted most for Christmas.

"Well, now," said the same beautifully cultured voice. "This is a delightful surprise."

"My uncle Jonas," Brice hissed in my ear.

"Do you have to stand so close?" I muttered.

Then I saw Jonas de Winter and almost fainted. No wonder Dom had been so gobsmacked when he saw that medieval slave merchant. Jonas was like the medieval guy's total twin! It was just like Lola said – these gangsters had been causing mayhem since the dawn of history.

Dom stood beside his uncle, looking defiant.

The door opened again and his mother swept in, in a gale of lovely perfume. "Oh, these must be Dom's little time-travellers!" she gushed. "What time do they come from again, Dominic?"

"You tell me, Mother," he muttered. "Since you know so much."

I felt Brice's breath tickle my ear. "OK, darling, you're on. This is your big moment. Just say exactly what I tell you."

I felt unpleasantly like a PODS glove puppet, but I obediently said my lines: "We've brought the device, but we're not handing it over until we're convinced that Dominic is free to go."

Unfortunately, I don't think I was very impressive because all the de Winters broke into tolerant smiles, like I was a little kid just playing at being grown-up.

"Free to go," repeated Dom's mother in a wondering tone. "But of course Dominic is free to go. What do you think we are, dear? Monsters?"

Jonas de Winter smiled. "Dom is free to leave this house any time he likes." He slung a casual arm around his nephew, and it was like a creepy action replay of the merchant with Stephen. "Just out of curiousity, dear boy," he said casually. "Where *will* you go?"

Dom's next words blew everyone away, including Brice.

"I'd like to go and live with my dad," he said stiffly.

The atmosphere instantly dropped way below zero.

Laura de Winter's beautiful face tightened like a mask. "Dominic, dear, I'm afraid you're a little confused," she said coldly. "Your father is dead, you know that."

He looked disgusted. "You people are unbelievable. Did you seriously think I'd never find out about Dad?"

Omigosh, I thought. Maybe little Dom isn't quite so helpless as everyone thought.

There was a stunned silence.

"Well," said Jonas de Winter. "If that's the case, of course you must go to be with your father. We understand perfectly, don't we, Laura?" And he totally released Dom from his embrace. He actually held his hands in the air so we could see he wasn't holding Dom against his will.

Dom strolled casually over to our side of the table. He was acting dead cool, but I could see he was trembling with strain.

Jonas beamed at us. "You see! All very civilised. But civilisation works both ways, my dears, so now you must keep your side of the bargain."

"Give them the device and get Dom out of here," Brice hissed.

I stared wildly round the room, trying to think of something, anything, which would get us out of this nightmare.

"Just *do* it, Melanie!" Brice threatened in my ear. "You're supposed to be saving Dom, remember?"

I will, I will, I thought. Just as soon as I figure out how.

Because no matter what Brice said, I knew I couldn't do it his way.

Just think about it. Generations of evil de Winters snaking in and out of eternity, buying and selling human lives, wrecking my lovely blue-green planet. And I'm supposed to trust these characters with the sacred keys of history? I don't *think* so!

If only our tags were still working, I thought desperately. We could send for Agency back-up, then we'd get these people sorted, no problem.

Then clear as day, I heard a voice inside my head.

It wasn't Michael or Mr Allbright. It wasn't anyone celestial, funnily enough. It was Des, my down-to-earth step-dad. I could actually see him, in my mind's eye. He was sitting in his favourite armchair and he was smiling at me. "Melanie," he said earnestly. "If you can't make it, then you've just got to fake it, girl."

I felt a prickle of excitement. My step-dad could have a point. Wasn't Mr Allbright always saying that imagination was a genuine angelic power? Then why not use it? If I tried to *imagine* I still had my personal hotline to the Agency, maybe it would come true?

Well, it was worth a shot. I felt furtively for my damaged tags.

"Excuse me you guys, if you're listening," I said silently. "We're trapped somewhere in the twenty-third century and we have a major problem. We've got to stop the de Winters wrecking history but we totally don't want to sacrifice this really great kid, Dominic. Please help us ASAP."

Did I feel a genuine tingle of angel electricity then, or was I just so desperate I wanted to believe it?

Jonas de Winter's voice was as soft as ever. "The device, if you please."

I made a major production out of it, slowly groping inside the wrong pocket of my jacket, then exploring the pockets of my jeans.

"Don't screw up now, sweetheart," Brice warned. "My brother's life is on the line here."

"So no pressure then," I muttered.

The headmaster's smile was becoming a little fixed. "I hope you aren't playing games with me, young lady."

My heart sank. I knew we'd finally run out of time. And not knowing what else to do, I miserably held out the device.

"Just push it across the table," he coaxed. "That's it, nice and easy. No sudden moves."

In agonising slow-mo I laid it on the table, and felt a collective quiver of excitement go through the de Winters.

My mates and I watched, hypnotised, as Jonas de Winter reached out.

I felt numb with horror. By the time this evil family had finished ransacking the past, Earth's future would be totally in their hands.

And it very nearly was. But then, unbelievably, Dom's mother broke the spell.

"You silly boy," she snapped. "You could have had everything, yet you gave it all up to be with that fool."

Dom went white with rage. Before anyone could stop him, he snatched up the device, frantically pressing keypads.

I heard Brice give a hiss of pure surprise.

Scribbles of neon light appeared in mid air.

The de Winters looked oddly fascinated. But under their studied calm, it was obvious they were terrified.

"NOW!" yelled Reuben.

Angel martial-arts teachers say that when you're in tune with the cosmos, you don't have to think about your moves, you just spring effortlessly into action. And that's exactly what we did.

For the first time in our training, my mates and I used angelic martial-arts skills on humans. Brice invisibly lent a helping hand. Dom and Lily pitched in. There was a brief, incredibly dramatic struggle which I'm happy to say we won.

Just minutes later we had them all neatly tied up with the pretty golden curtain ropes.

I almost cried with relief. Against all the odds and with absolutely *no* back-up, unless you count that inspired advice from my lovely step-dad, we had done it. Impossible as it seemed, we'd saved Dom *and* history!!

Reuben clapped Dom on the back. "Nice work, mate. Now give us that device, before someone really gets hurt."

Dom shook his head. "No way! This is payback time."

Uh-oh, I thought. My mates and I exchanged startled glances.

Dom had a weird sleepwalking expression, as if he couldn't believe this was finally happening.

"You know what I hate about you people?" he said. I saw that he had tears glittering in his eyes. "Your kids are just like cute little pets to you. You buy us expensive clothes, send us to be educated in your special Phoenix schools. And all the time, you're filling our heads with your disgusting lies. I've been on to you for years, Uncle Jonas. And you, Mum. You think you've been watching me, when all the time I've been watching you."

"Dom," I said gently.

"Oh, don't worry, I'm not going to kill them," Dom said earnestly. "I just want them to suffer, the way they've made people suffer for centuries. And now I've come up with the perfect punishment."

He laughed. "You thought it was hilarious, didn't you? Funny little Dom, so naïve, he'd actually use a powerful cosmic device to run some sad little time scam for pocket money. Yeah, right!"

"You little toad!" said Jonas in a startled voice. "You were running scientific trials all along!"

"Correct, Uncle Jonas! I was also getting an excellent education. I saw a boy succeed where the grown-ups had screwed up. In thirteenth-century France I saw a boy inspire thousands of other kids to follow him, not out of fear or for money or because the de Winters yanked their strings. But out of pure love."

"That's highly commendable, dear—" his mother interrupted.

"Just shut up and listen!" Dom yelled. He drew a shaky breath, then went on in a quieter voice, "So I figured, hey, I get it! We really can have Heaven on Earth like everyone says. Except that Stephen made one big mistake. He forgot about the dark side. But I won't do that. I've been watching them operate my whole life. That's why I had to perfect the device, so I can get rid of my family."

"Dom," said Lola. "Maybe, this isn't—"

But Dom wasn't listening. "The only thing is where to send you," he pondered. "Personally I'd love to zap you all back to Marseilles and put you on your own ancestors' slave ships. Poetic justice, don't you think?"

He laughed.

"But then it might be even more fun to zap you forwards, to one of those experimental space colonies they're planning to build in our future. That way, you wouldn't even be contaminating the same planet as the rest of the human race."

I was getting a wee bit concerned at this point, to be honest. Don't get me wrong. I totally sympathised with Dominic's feelings. But as you know, the Agency doesn't exactly encourage violent acts of revenge.

But like all de Winters, once Dom got going, he seemed kind of unstoppable. He pointed to the madly twirling time FX. "See that, you guys? In twenty seconds max, you'll be gone for ever."

"He won't do it," his mother said scornfully. "He's all talk like his father."

Dom's face twisted. I'm not exaggerating, he looked totally desperate. He swung round, deliberately aiming the device at the captives. All the relatives ducked, whimpering with fright. I think that's when we all realised that Dom wasn't playing around. He really meant to do it.

"He's completely out of control," Lola whispered.

Reuben's voice rang out like a bell. "This won't work, Dom! You can't create Paradise by just *deleting* all your enemies, man."

But I knew it had all gone too far. It was like Dom didn't *dare* to stop now. His fingers flickered to the keypad and with no expression whatsoever, he activated the device.

There was a collective flinch of horror. I felt totally helpless. But there was nothing we could do except wait to see what happened next.

Apparently Dom had decided to zap the de Winters to that space station after all, because when they appeared, the new time FX were lovelier and more futuristic than ever. Unbelievably beautiful colours filled the room, but at their core was a light so pure and unearthly, that my eyes filled with tears.

My step-dad's advice had worked. Our Agency back-up had arrived in the nick of time.

The light levels adjusted and Michael stepped into the room, closely followed by several other agents.

He calmly took the device from Dom.

"Reuben's right. This is not the way," he told Dom. "The power to judge and punish does not belong to you. If you really want to change the world, you have to understand that."

Dom looked completely awed. I don't think he had any idea his uncle's boardroom was full of angels. I think he just took them for humans from some wonderful far distant future.

Forgetting that we'd ever been enemies, I whispered eagerly to the invisible Brice, "Isn't this brilliant? You finally kept your promise! You saved Dom!"

At least that's what I was going to say.

But he had silently slipped away. Later it occurred to me that he totally couldn't face Michael.

I noticed Michael watching me with his lovely all-seeing eyes. "Actually, you all saved Dom," he said gravely. "His father is a good influence and now Dom will have his true guardian angel to watch over him. Though the truth is, we never stopped watching over him, you know, Melanie. Not even for a moment."

He seemed to think we could leave it at that, but my mind swirled with unanswered questions. OK, so Dom was safe. But what about Brice? I wanted to ask. Where's *his* happy ending? Is anyone watching over him? Can he break his bargain with the PODS and come back home now that Dom's safe? Or has he just blown it with you guys for all Eternity?

Michael passed his hand lightly over my hair, and I felt about a zillion archangel volts sizzle down my spine. "Go home," he repeated softly. "We'll take care of this from now on."

# CHAPTER ELEVEN

A few days later my phone jolted me out of a really deep sleep.

"Melanie speaking," I mumbled.

"Sorry if I woke you," said Michael's amused voice.

I shot up in bed like a rocket. "No problem, I'll be down at the Agency in two ticks," I promised groggily.

I caught sight of myself in the mirror. With my bed hair sticking up all over the place, I looked exactly like a cockatoo.

"Oh, didn't I say? I'm at Guru," he said cheerfully. "I've been at the Agency all night. I thought we could have a chat over breakfast."

I carefully replaced the phone.

Then I registered what he'd said and practically went into orbit, madly throwing on the first clothes which tumbled out of my wardrobe.

"Omigosh, omigosh," I moaned."I can't believe he wants to see me by myself."

There could only be one explanation for this exclusive invitation.

My cosmic crimes had caught up with me at last. I was going to be reprimanded big-time.

As I walked into Guru, Michael waved from a booth.

"I ordered some rather delicious looking pastries. Hope that's OK?" he said.

But when our food came, I couldn't manage a mouthful, just sat fiddling nervously with my cutlery. My heart was thumping so hard, I was sure Michael must be able to hear it. Why didn't he get it over with and put me out of my misery?

"If it's about the tags, maybe I could just pay the Agency back or something," I blurted out.

Michael looked blank. "The tags?"

"We didn't plan to materialise," I said desperately. "It was an accident."

Michael poured me some freshly squeezed orange juice. "A very useful accident as it turned out," he said serenely.

I was totally bewildered. When was I going to get my ticking off?

"Oh, did you hear the good news?" he added. "Orlando's team saved about fifty of those brave young Crusaders."

I felt a pang of distress. OK, so it was better than nothing, but I'd wanted all the kids to be saved.

Michael gave me one of his looks. "At the Agency, we believe in evolution," he said gently. "So we try to take the long-term view."

I took a sip of juice. I got the definite feeling he was working up to something.

"That's the marvellous thing about Eternity," he said. "There's no need to rush. Forests turn into diamonds. Evil changes into good. Sometimes whole centuries go by before you even begin to see the big picture."

I had a funny feeling we'd moved on from evolution. In fact I thought Michael might actually be answering my questions about Brice, but I wasn't quite sure.

"Erm," I said, "did I do something wrong? Did I break another cosmic law, you know, by co-operating with a fallen..." I'd started playing nervously with my hair, a sure sign I'm stressed.

"No, Melanie," Michael said firmly. "You played your part perfectly."

I stared at him. "Really?"

I thought I might cry with relief.

"Really. So do you think you could help me out with these pastries now? There seem to be rather a lot." Michael sounded so plaintive, that I truly wanted to hug him. Imagine an archangel worrying about his waistline!

"I'd love to," I said truthfully. "It's just, this is a really busy day for me."

He gave me a delighted smile. "Of course, Lola's party."

I stood up to go. "I don't mean to be rude, but after last time, I want everything to be perfect," I explained shyly.

"Just one thing." My heart turned over. Michael sounded deadly serious. "Next time you see a worm hole, please don't feel you have to jump through it. Perhaps you might like to pass that message on to the others?"

Just in time, I saw that his eyes were twinkling. I went weak at the knees. Michael's such a tease sometimes.

Mo caught me up at the door. "Who knows, maybe she'll actually get to open it this time!" He gave me back my parcel.

I slapped his palm. "See you later, yeah?"

"Wouldn't miss it for the world," he beamed.

But as I hurried out into the early morning streets, I don't think I was completely awake. Because for the first time ever, I had this moment of pure clairvoyance, a vision almost, like I was being shown a movie preview of Lola's party.

Everything was going brilliantly. The DJ was cool. The music was hot. Fairy lights twinkled in the trees and I was dancing with my mates under a big fat moon. Any time now, Orlando would step out of the shadows, and tell me what a great job I'd done in the twenty-third century.

But at this moment my soul-mate was boogeying up to me, proudly wearing my present to her.

"Do you really like it, Lollie?" I asked anxiously. "I can take it back, you know."

"Are you kidding!" she said. "This isn't a T-shirt, babe. It's our cosmic mission statement!"

She leaped into the air, giving a cheeky cheerleader twirl as she came down, and for an instant I saw the message glittering on her T-shirt. Two words which for me and Lola, totally sum up what being an angel is all about.

### *Flying High*